Little Sister

Joan Westerman

BALBOA.
PRESS
A DIVISION OF HAY HOUSE

Balboa Press books may be ordered through booksellers or by contacting:

Balboa Press
A Division of Hay House
1663 Liberty Drive
Bloomington, IN 47403
www.balboapress.com.au
1-(877) 407-4847

ISBN: 978-1-4525-0967-9 (sc)
ISBN: 978-1-4525-0968-6 (e)

Printed in the United States of America

Balboa Press rev. date: 04/04/2013

To Briar

for the laughter

and

Jo, Finn, Eleanor, Tom and Oliver

thank you

Sometimes it doesn't take a lot to tip you over into somewhere else. For Jess it was the email. Just a simple message but unexpected all the same. Damn she was angry!

Your sister has let you go and it's time you got the monkey off your back.

Who the hell are you to tell me what I should and shouldn't do she screamed? Damned right I should get the monkey off my back but guess what? It's my goddamned monkey not yours so there!

Monkey monkey let go let go.

The anger came at her from nowhere and Jess cursed the fact that she let it in at all. She knew she should do better but it felt like a toothache that wouldn't go away.

The fumes of futility curled slowly through her skull as she tried to block out the past. But it's too late. Jess is caught once more. Trapped.

Families. Bloody hell.

Three sisters. Related by blood but all so different. Right from the start Jess felt like an outsider in the family. Lost in another zone. Spinning away beyond their reach. Their world.

Not mine, no never.

Jess was very young when she first became aware of tension and family conflict. Of course she couldn't put it into words at that stage apart from the odd howled protest that fell on deaf ears anyway in the brick house on the hill. Perhaps she sensed long before then that she was different to the others. Her family. Sisters brother parents. Grandparents she didn't remember. Too old when she was too young.

Her earliest thoughts and memories were mere snatches of human contact with others who were supposed to be related. Sisters who shared her bedroom and made life a misery. Took all that belonged to Jess and ruined every waking moment with their torment and teasing. Laughed at her poked her prodded her ordered her round. Called Jess names and told her she was the baby. Hated her just for sharing their world.

I tried so hard so hard to please them but it was never enough.

Jess's mother was overrun with her own secret world of fear and dread and insecurity and household chores. Four young children and a selfish husband. No car. No income of her own. No friends. And an overbearing mother and invalid father to care for as well. Holding it all together for the sake of the children at such a cost to herself in the end. Keeping all her worries inside and being the stoic one the martyr the brave young wife and mother and daughter. For what?

The ghosts were always there though weren't they May?

Snatches and images of Jess's childhood soar back to her haltingly to remind her of something lost. What it is that sends them now?

Step on a crack you'll marry a . . . .

The childhood chants seem foreign to Jess now but it wasn't always so. Now they are just words. No longer correct or proper.

Jess cringes at the memories and a small grin bubbles to the surface from somewhere deep within. The child. The little girl with the white hair who asked for nothing from her family and got nothing in return.

Little sister little sister, baby, baby!

Time has slipped past Jess like the breeze that rattles through the clotheslines of her childhood. Somehow that all seems like another world. Another life. Not hers.

And Jess *was* the little sister all those years ago in the brick house at the top of the street. Her mother said she almost killed her in childbirth, so maybe she was right to be indifferent. To treat Jess with disdain. But it was hardly her fault that the delivery was difficult was it?

Jess was a big baby. The fourth child.

Is this your baby May oh she's so cute isn't she?

The trouble was Jess never *felt* cute in that household. Or loved or wanted or cared for emotionally. She felt like an alien.

From her first conscious moments Jess dreamed of being discovered by her *real* family and taken back to where she belonged. There must have been a mix-up at the hospital she decided. Jess didn't even look like the others, all so dark and swarthy. Where did her fair complexion and white hair come from? Jess wanted to know.

Blondie blondie don't go in the sun you'll burn.

But she didn't listen anyway. Jess went outdoors as often as she could to get away from the family that she felt sure wasn't hers.

May was the youngest of four children. She was the little sister too. Her brothers were the favourites even though May was the only daughter. They were a working class family but May's mother had aspirations of greatness for her offspring. At least for the boys anyway.

But not for her only daughter.

May was only sixteen when she was unceremoniously moved out of her room to make way for a boarder. The extra income was needed to help educate the boys. They would become doctors, while May trained for nursing. May's course in life was set by her mother and she didn't question it. She was already the dutiful daughter.

The sand was hot and harsh between Jess's toes but she loved it anyway.

The sea oh the sea let me splash and run in the saltspray.

Jess counted each and every day of her childhood by the sea. She breathed the salt air and wallowed in the curl of the shoreline. She hunted for treasures in the rockpools. Jess ran with the wind and lay drying on the hot sand listening to the ships and the gulls and watching the racing clouds. It was in her blood but she didn't know that then. Only that it *was*.

Jess knew that without the sea she would be lost forever.

She sucked in every breath of salt air as though her life depended on it and maybe it did. Who knows how things would have turned out otherwise?

It was up to May really, all those days on the beach. It was in her blood too, and her father's before her. But Jess didn't discover such things till years later. Many years later, when she was ready.

It was May who had the sea in her veins, not her husband Arthur. He was from England and used to the cold and damp, not the warm sun and the waves and the joy of the sea.

A strange pairing Jess often thought later in life. Such opposites her parents. Such different backgrounds. Different worlds.

So I guess I should be grateful to May after all mused Jess, even though I had almost caused her mortal injury during my rude entry into this life.

May always said to respect your elders and be obedient and talk when you are spoken to, but Jess learned very early that spoken words in the brick house were usually fraught with hidden danger and double meanings and mixed messages. Words spoken were words that couldn't be retrieved no matter how hard you tried. So Jess learned not to say too many. She harvested them in her head and saved them for better times.

Baby baby she can't talk!

But Jess *did* talk. She held conversations and invented fantasies. She created great adventures to help her through childhood.

It was her world of words that kept her smiling through the loneliness that surrounded her in this strange family.

I can talk I can, but not to you!

Jess gazed through the stained glass window and wondered how it had all come to this. Where did all those years go and why had half her life vanished since she was the small white-haired child?

She clasped her chin and dived into the void of memories that sat heavy in her skull. She tried to make some sense of it all. She wanted answers.

May didn't question her mother when she was relegated to the back verandah as a teenager. Gone was her own small refuge in the Newcastle home. Her tiny space now came with thick canvas blinds that barely kept out the cold drafty winds that blew in from the sea or the noises of the street on the long hot summer nights when May would swelter as she tried to sleep. The bedroom that had until recently been hers was now occupied by a stranger, but if May was put out by this she never showed it.

Stiff upper lip there there May her mother always said and respect your elders that's a good girl.

May would not dream of disobeying her mother. She accepted with tough stoicism that fate had dealt her such treatment because she had been born a girl. She was the only female in the household besides her mother, and as such it fell to her to perform many of the menial tasks and chores of the household while her brothers got on with their lives and their education. The pattern of May's life was set by her mother and involved the intrusion of other lives and rules the older woman established in the family home.

But Jess often wondered what had happened inside May's head all those years ago? Did May feel resentful of her lot as she lay in her narrow bed out there on the back verandah while the boys were all safely inside? Did she resent the fact that she was seemingly less-deserving because of her gender? Did May ever face her own demons and feel *angry?*

The tide of Jess's life tugs relentlessly. She is caught at the edge of the eddy. Waves of anxiety slap against her there in the swirling waters and she can't seem to shake free.

Queenie queenie who's got the ball?

Jess's heart lurches suddenly as she recalls the hours of games with her sisters. Forced and fragile. Terrifying at times. Blindfolded.

Tread on a crack and you'll . . . .

The cursor flashes on the screen and Jess is back in control. She is safe now. The years apart have seen to that. But it wasn't always so.

The three girls run ahead of their mother down to the bus stop.

Wait for me wait for me!

They are clean and tidy and freshly dressed in matching yellow frocks made by their mother with a different transfer on each pocket. Shiny hair and shiny shoes. Ready for town.

And woe betide you if you get dirty!

Woe betide. Woebetide woebetide.

Jess used to think it was just one word like some of mother's other words.

Transmogrify.

I'll transmogrify you if you do that!

When Jess was little her skin used to crawl and she'd hide under the bed just imagining what that meant. It was utterly terrifying. She had a way with words, her mother.

I suppose in a way that's all May had. Everything else had been taken away gradually and lost in the daily ritual of her life over the years. But Jess never did fully understand the fierce loyalty and devotion May showed to her own mother, who by all accounts was as hard as nails and ruthless to boot.

May would spend her days tending to the house and the garden and her children in that order and Jess assumed she led a fairly peaceful if somewhat restless existence in those days. Outwardly at least everything was calm and ordered and neat but in her head things must have been very different. Not that she ever talked about herself much, hardly ever in fact. Even in the later years when she had become the white-haired one.

No no I can't tell you that I'll take it to the grave with me.

And she did of course and what's the sense of that?

Jess never really got to know her as a person. She didn't share her dreams and loves and thoughts and desires and disappointments.

No it simply wasn't done. May saw to that.

The bus pulls into the kerb. Jess is filled with excitement and anticipation but she stands quietly near her mother and looks down at her shoes awkwardly, not wanting to give too much away. She has already learned that to show emotion or joy or fear or uncertainty is a weakness that can bring you undone and earn scorn and wrath, so young Jess stands silent and patient on the street corner.

It's a game that she plays where she has total control. Jess has the words in her head where they are safe. Nobody knows her secret. Especially *them*. The two older sisters.

Queenie queenie I've got the ball. Hahahaha.

Hannah pushes Jess in the back and forces her into the bus. May ignores this and pays the bus driver while Jess waits patiently for her chance to escape upstairs to her favourite seat at the front. She gets away from the sisters and slithers along the cool green leather to her corner.

Jess sits tightly and leans carefully against the steel bus as the motor revs and the bus pulls out into the city traffic. The world rolls by and Jess is transfixed. It is wonderful being here away from the house on the hill.

She begins writing stories in her head. Beautiful and adventurous stories where there are no mean sisters.

Once upon a time there was a little girl and she . . . .

Sometimes I don't think it really matters where you start or what brings on a change thought Jess.

Sometimes it's too late anyway to analyse things. They just happen.

That's how it was this time for Jess when she got that damn email. Something inside just snapped and a voice in her head called out *enough*.

Nothing earth-shattering she knew. But it mattered.

It was as though there was sudden clarity in Jess's life. All the years of family frustration surfaced as she gazed in disbelief at the monitor. Amazing really. Why hadn't she seen it coming?

Jess wondered why she had held on to the threads of an illusion for so long. Why had she pretended that the family-thing would work out with time? Who was she kidding after all these years?

Paper . . . . Scissors . . . . rock.

Wham!

. . . families!

Jess glanced around the office and saw only photos of the dead. Not the living. Except for her own two children. Why is that? Where are the sisters?

Baby baby hahaha.

Maybe it was time anyway for the cleansing and the email just put it into words. Finally.

Let go let go let go.

But it's *me* in control now not them protested Jess. My life my turn my choice. Not theirs any more. I'm the one letting go now and damn it feels good!

Come here baby do this baby, go away and hide till we call you baby, hahah!

Now it's my turn to let go. The dreams the hopes the false pretence of a family that never was. The lies the teasing the bullying the ruins.

Let go let go!

May frowned as Jess ran up to her along the beach. She held out her latest treasure from the rockpools. A coloured starfish.

The sparkle and smell of the sea filled Jess's body.

Look look she cries eagerly to her mother. But either she didn't hear or didn't *want* to hear, for she turned away from the small white-haired girl. Jess sighed as she lay there on the hot summer sand. She felt the sting of rejection. A family that didn't really want her.

Go away child go away can't you see I'm busy.

But Jess is still excited by the starfish and demanding of her mother. May continues to ignore her. A tiny piece of Jess breaks off and washes out with the waves there on the shore of her favourite beach.

She doesn't understand the games adults play but she has already absorbed the hurt.

Sit down child and be quiet and speak when you are spoken to.

May never questioned her lack of life choices. It simply *was*. She just put aside her hopes and dreams and got on with life.

May accepted that her brothers were more deserving of an education than she for hadn't her mother always told her that's how it was? She already knew that she was cut out for a different life. Marriage and raising children and caring for a husband and household. Just as her mother had done.

If she resented it at all it never showed. May had been trained not to show her feelings from an early age.

There there May don't get upset think of king and country and be a good girl for mother.

May had been taught that her choices were restricted because she was a girl. That was how it was and May accepted her lot without question. She didn't cry foul or bleat about injustice. May simply followed her mother's orders and did what was expected of her in the humble Newcastle home.

Jess slinks away from the group on the beach. Her family.

She retreats to the rockpool world to create her own life. Images and words spin into stories in her head and she is alone and content and happy. There is only the blueness of the sky and the sea and the dazzling saltspray.

Sssssss . . . . sssssss . . . . swoosh.

Jess plays games in her head as she searches for sea creatures and beautiful tiny shells. She is smiling inside. She can no longer hear the demanding voices of her sisters and mother for they have ceased to exist. Their harsh cries are replaced by silence except for the sounds of the sea. Noone can take this away from Jess. Not even *them*.

I'm not a baby, I'm not I'm not!

Far away up the beach the shadowy figure of her brother scrambles amongst the boulders by the breakwater. He is not part of the group even though he belongs by birth. The only boy till the little brother is born much later on. The odd one out with this group of women. How Jess envies him and marvels at his freedom. His isolation. His maleness and sense of adventure. Lucky luck lucky.

Sometimes even though the sky is clear and blue and the sun is shining outside Jess's heart feels heavy and she wonders why that is.

Take today for example. A normal Autumn day with beautiful clear skies. You would think that should make me smile and feel happy but it doesn't thinks Jess. She wishes it did.

Jess digs round in the cluttered garden of her skull to unearth the cause of her malaise. Nothing helps. She strolls outside and sits by the small pool, soaking in the warmth. But still clouds descend.

Go away go away!

Back at the computer the plastic flip flop plant from Japan is going crazy in the filtered light. Jess smiles at it's simplicity and a tiny bubble of joy breaks free within. Maybe her mood is lifting after all.

The clock ticks impatiently and breaks her concentration. Jess is once more thrown off-key. She tries to focus on the words but it is difficult. Her mind wanders back to those years where the journey began.

I don't want to go there. Not now.

Weddings and funerals. That's when families get together, isn't it? Birthdays and Christmases. Maybe. But not for Jess.

Not even the wedding was enough this time and Jess was pissed off!

Her only son and the sisters couldn't even be bothered to show.

Last time she'd seen them come to think of it *was* a funeral.

James. The remaining brother. Gone. Such a different life he led didn't he? But he was still flesh and blood. Still related by birth. Older but no wiser. Yet Jess could still feel his presence.

G'day Curl howareya eh?

Angry. That's what I feel.

Where does the anger come from?

Jess's clinical self tells her to beware. The anger is not healthy. She knows that. But the emotional part, the child, tells her it's o.k. She's earned it. Damn right!

Sit still when I tell you, don't move, come here, nonono.

May was never too sure why she'd chosen Arthur. Perhaps it was the Depression. Perhaps it was her mother who at first glance hadn't approved of him at all.

No no May you're far too good for him!

Or maybe it was just one of those split second decisions that sometimes come out of nowhere. May didn't remember why she'd chosen Arthur instead of Harold. Somehow it had just happened. And now it was too late.

May loved him of course but she'd loved Harold too. And they'd had such *fun* together. She and Harold. Riding in the back of the Bakers Cart on the hot summer nights of her twenties. Giggling and holding hands and kissing furtively as the old horse clip-clopped along the dusty streets.

Harold had given her the power of freedom and the gift of joy. He had loved her in the purest fashion.

But Arthur had loved her too and wooed her with words and romance and promise. May had been taken in by his earnestness. His entreaties of love. His smouldering passion.

Poor May. It was so confusing. She had such strong feelings for them both. It was a real dilemna. What should she do?

Bossy boots. That was Hannah. Jess's older sister. Always demanding this and that.

What did I do to deserve that?

Nothing. I was the baby of the family that's all thought Jess. Maybe that alone was the reason. But that was hardly my fault was it? An accident of birth was all it was and I had no say in the matter, did I?

Happiness is a fleeting thing. It hangs on such a slender thread doesn't it? Happy childhoods are even rarer. Jess knew. Believe me, she knew.

Baby baby you're such a baby!

The anger rose to the surface again. Jess surveyed it as an adult. She attempted to put it in context.

But the part of her that was wounded all those years ago by indifference just can't let it slide away into nothingness. It seems so unfair.

I *do* have a right to be angry Jess yelled. To feel the pain and the hurt and the injustice meted out by the older siblings and mother and absent father.

Her friends over the years talked about their own happy childhoods and Jess never understood what they meant. It seemed like a fantasy. Jess had never *felt* what her friends had.

All she had left of her childhood were snatches of memories. Scatterings that mostly she didn't even recognise as belonging to her. Images and pictures. Fragments that passed her by in the long lonely silences of her childhood. Jess didn't remember much of it.

There must be a reason why that is so.

But what is it? Why had she hidden her childhood?

May married Arthur in a small drab ceremony attended by family and a few nursing colleagues. Arthur had finally pressed her into a choice. Him or Harold. He would have it no other way. May had to decide he'd said.

So May went ahead and chose Arthur, swept away by his Englishness and his tireless pursuit. She abandoned her darling Harold and tried to put the joy and laughter out of her head. Life was a serious business was it not? That's what May's mother had always told her and May was not about to argue with her now.

Besides, the old woman had come round to preferring Arthur hadn't she? He had slowly endeared himself to May's mother, who took his haughty English ways at face value and assumed therefore that Arthur had "class." As such he could provide an air of something exotic she mused. A touch of respectability for May and thus for the family as well. It never occurred to her that it was all show. That Arthur was from working stock like herself. That indeed he would soon be unemployed due to the Depression and would remain so for the next five years.

Jess paused at the keyboard and searched in her head for pieces to the puzzle of her past. She knew they would not easily be found. Why was it so difficult to recall any happiness?

Go to your room and don't fuss, your father will see you when he's ready.

Blank. Perhaps she has deliberately erased it all long ago?

Little things come back to Jess but they are not much.

A yellow dress. A teaset. Her doll with the beautiful golden hair.

Mummy mummy she cut off Janie's hair!

Nothing was totally Jess's in the house on the hill, *they* saw to that. So it didn't matter if she had treasures or special rocks or dolls or a teaset.

They took them and made them their own.

But they couldn't take her world of words could they?

I hate them I hate them and I hate this house!

Jess sits in the spa at the local pool. The sickly chlorine invades her senses and makes her eyes smart. Bubbles foam and churn around her.

Jess is stuck in a hot pool of white dross. Her life is oozing out of her. She is being sucked into the maelstrom. She is adrift.

Go away we don't want to play with you go away go away.

In her mind Jess sees the two sisters. Their faces are before her in the steam and the bubbles. Staring. Silent and dumb.

Were they really part of my life or did I just imagine it?

Wake up Jess it's time for school hurry hurry.

Jess sinks lower in the spa so that the water jet shoots up behind her. She is momentarily distracted. Warmth seeps through her body and she relaxes.

Her mind drifts back to the waters of her life.

The rock pools of her childhood. The bogey hole. The sea baths.

Nobbies beach, Newcastle. Coogee beach, Sydney.

The Fernery, Frankston. St Kilda, Venus Bay, Manly, Bondi, Clovelly, Maroubra, Cowes, Pt Fairy, Cottesloe, Broome, Waikiki, Gulf of Mexico, Greenmount, Woolamai, Smiths Beach, Torquay, Norman Bay, Ningaloo, Yepoon, Cape Patterson, Mission Bay, Bay of Islands.

Water. Always water. It is part of her soul.

The little girl ran and ran along the beach and as she ran a weird thing happened. The sea became her and she became the sea. Strange that it should be so, but it was. At least that's how she thought it was all those years ago. The sea. *Her* sea. Her world.

Swish, swish, sssss.

As a young child Jess felt the sea creep into her bones and take hold of her. Care for her. Nourish her soul. It was as though it became her friend for a reason, and Jess treasured every moment.

I suppose that's one thing that I have mother to thank for, Jess recollected. She loved the sea too. It was definitely in the family.

But even down at the seaside Jess couldn't escape the sisters for long. *They* always came too. Pity. It would have been so much nicer without them.

Look out for your little sister will you and see that she doesn't come to any harm there's good girls.

They didn't suspect that Jess could take care of herself. Didn't want them or need them even then. *Especially* then.

She just wanted to be alone to spin her words into magic.

Once upon a time . . . .

The photos adorning the office wall tell Jess that she belongs somewhere. But it wasn't always so.

They show smiling faces of friends and family. Jess's family. Not the sisters. No, not them.

Her mother and father and brothers and aunt and father-in-law and mother-in law are there too. Captured in colour and framed in wood.

Jess scans their faces but she cannot reach them now for they are all dead.

She has the memories but wonders if that is enough.

Other people have families still alive and sometimes Jess is jealous. Her partner has her mother and brothers still. Despite the distance.

She is perplexed that her family are gone when she is only mid-way.

Jess cannot change it she knows. She accepts what is. But still there are times when it causes angst and catches her out. She feels the aloneness at the strangest times. A stroll round the garden brings back Arthur, her father. The sea brings back her mother, May. She sees her down the corridor of time splashing in the waves on Newcastle beach. A ride on Jess's motor scooter brings back her favourite brother Paul. She sees his young face laughing. It seems senseless that he crashed and died at twenty one. Sometimes the pain of that night jabs at Jess's soul and she feels the waste afresh.

Gone. All gone.

The battered photo box is almost hidden from view in Jess's spare room. It is dusty and frayed. Tatty round the edges.

Jess doesn't know what made her seek it out this morning. Perhaps she wants clues. Pieces of the puzzle. Images of her family.

She bends down and scoops the box from the shelf. Almost too harshly. Perhaps she is a little afraid of the contents.

But why should she be bothered by the haunting half-smiles and the sepia ghosts within?

Frustrated by her own short-comings Jess plops the box heavily onto the laminex table. The cardboard lid is askew. It has seen better days. Perhaps it is a little like me Jess muses.

But she doesn't want to get side-tracked. She needs some answers. Surely the faces in the photos will offer up *something*. Won't they?

Jess is still feeling apprehensive as she pushes aside the lid and reaches inside the box. She's seen these images so many times in her life already. But not for a long time now. They have been relegated to obscurity. Hidden away. Banished from her world.

Jess pauses briefly and wonders if the sisters still have family pictures. She supposes they must. Where are they now?

Come here child and stand still for the camera and woebetide you if . . . .

Why are we moving mummy and where are we going to live now?

The small white-haired girl glanced at her mother as she started to pack up the house. Jess's home. The tall house on the hill.

Jess wondered why they were suddenly leaving. Was it her fault? Was it something she'd done?

Daddy has a new job in Sydney so we are going to live there now.

Where's Sydney? Doesn't daddy like his job at the steelworks any more?

Hush now child and stop asking so many questions.

Look after your sister now and take her out to play while I pack will you Hannah there's a good girl, mummy's busy. Nononono! I don't want to go with Hannah!

Jess is dragged outside and Hannah marches her round the corner. Off down the street. Jess's silent howls of protest crash to the concrete path.

She feels leaden and beaten as though soon she too will be dashed against the concrete path. Noone will save her from the bossy sister.

They never do. Jess knows.

Paper . . . scissors . . . rock.

Jess holds herself tight inside as she follows Hannah down the hill.

Soon Hannah will start the game and Jess will have to obey. Hannah always makes up games but the rules never stay the same.

The only constant is that Hannah is always the winner and Jess is the loser. That's how it is. Jess can never defeat Hannah for she is older and stronger.

But in her head Jess is so much smarter and she *can* win.

Smarty pants smarty pants I've got the ball!

We're going to play hide and seek so sit down there and cover your eyes and count to one hundred Hannah suddenly demands. She runs off shrieking with laughter. Jess knows not to open her eyes. Hannah will come back and whack her good and proper. Jess stands still on the spot and listens to the sounds of the neighbourhood. Slowly she begins to count.

One two buckle my shoe, three four knock at the . . . .

Hannah has gone.

Ninety-nine, one hundred!

But to Jess's surprise Hannah is standing there right in front of her. She lets out a loud whoopee as Jess sees her.

I should have known she'd change the rules again.

But of course Hannah doesn't let Jess win.

She's playing a different game now.

Close your eyes again and I'll lead you down the street to somewhere really special and lovely Hannah says.

Jess doesn't like it but she knows better than to protest to Hannah. So the new game begins.

Jess suddenly hears the phone ring. She is startled. How long had she been staring at the photo of May?

As she picks up the hands free it stops ringing. Of course.

Damn phone, wouldn't you just know it?

The picture of May is still in her hand as Jess returns to the spare room.

A young woman's face stares up from the paper. Haunting. Almost smiling but not quite. Strong and determined. But fragile too.

It is a black and white print. Faded over the years. Slightly damaged.

That's what happened to May too . . . didn't it?

But the woman in the photo is so attractive and vibrant and full of promise. Her eyes have a sparkle. Her manner is jaunty. May. So young.

Is that really my mother thinks Jess?

Hannah walks fast and Jess's little legs struggle to keep up with her.

It's not far from here Hannah says. On they go. Hannah leads and Jess follows. Of course.

They cross the road at the bottom of the hill. Jess knows they are out of bounds already. May would not let them go this far without her.

But it will do Jess no good to protest. Hannah will hear none of it. She sets her own rules. Even May won't fight Hannah most of the time. Hannah knows. She is daddy's favourite.

The two sisters reach the end of the lane. Hannah suddenly stops. Here we are she shrieks.

Five six pick up sticks . . . .

Jess smells something strange and sickly. It invades her nostrils and she almost vomits. But Jess knows that Hannah will be cross with her if she shows weakness. She will be punished.

Jess stays very still. Her eyes are closed.

You can open your eyes when I count to three Hannah says. Jess hears Hannah giggle to herself but she doesn't pay any attention to that. Hannah is always giggling.

One . . . two . . . three!

Hannah shoves Jess towards the smell and runs away hooting with glee. Jess open her eyes wide. A dead cat! Decomposed and disgusting. Yuk!

One day you'll pay for this Hannah . . . one day! I hate you I hate you!

Jess stands there. She is frozen to the spot. But she doesn't protest or call out for it would be useless. Hannah would seek revenge. She always does.

Jess waits patiently for Hannah to return. She knows that Hannah will have to take her back home soon. Before mother gets angry.

That's how it is in the big brick house where Jess lives.

But some day it won't be will it Jess fumes . . . . *paper . . . scissors . . . . rock.*

Jess is crossing the bridge over the Barwon River when a sudden wind gust almost knocks her down. She reaches for the steel railing and hangs on. She is momentarily blinded by dust. It fills her eyes and nostrils. The river below is grey and stormy. Jess is dragged back fifty years to the shipyards and the sea and winter days in Newcastle.

Mother has taken Jess down to the docks to meet the prawn trawlers. The sisters are there too. Jess jumps up and down eagerly on the spot. She tries not to show her excitement but it is too hard. Jess cannot keep still.

Be still child May shouts above the din as she grabs Jess roughly by the shoulder. May clutches Jess nearer so that she is still for a brief moment. But not for long.

Mother mother here comes the trawler!

Jess knows that the fishermen will give her some free prawns when they unload.

Look at me look at me I am here!

But noone looks and noone comes and noone listens, for Jess is the baby. The little one. The smallest. They all ignore her.

But suddenly one of the fishermen holds out some prawns. Just for Jess.

Here you are little girl these are for you. She's so sweet isn't she, just like my little Rosie back home. What's your name little girl?

Jess reaches up to take hold of the gift, but her sister has other ideas.

Of course.

But they are mine, he said so didn't he? He gave them to ME!

May turns away and ignores what is happening there on the wharf with her two daughters, so that Hannah wins again. Jess tries not to cry or show any feeling. But inside she is hurting and angry with Hannah.

Jess starts the game again. The winning game. And because Hannah doesn't know she can't take the victory away.

Hahaha bossyboots, I win this time, ha ha!

Jess watches May's face to see if she has noticed any of this. But May has that familiar far-away look set on her brow. Jess knows she will not chastise

Hannah because she is a little afraid of her. May knows that Hannah is Arthur's favourite and she tries not to upset her too much. She knows that Hannah will go running to her father as soon as he walks in the door after work with all her stories and adventures of the day. Life is hard enough for May in the brick house on the hill so why would she make it any more difficult? No, best just let things be and get on with things as best she can. Keep the peace at all costs. That's the way!

Harry Harry where are you?

In all those long years of her growing up Jess never did hear May laugh too much. Not with her children. Not with Arthur either for that matter.

May said Harry had courted her before she met dad and wanted to be with her, but dad made her choose.

Him or me, he'd said. And for some strange reason mum chose Arthur. Funny that, she said years later. Long after Arthur had died of a brain tumour at the age of sixty four. Why didn't I choose Harry she wondered aloud? He was such fun and May had really liked him.

Well I guess there's no accounting for some of the choices we make thought Jess. But she sometimes wondered how different her life might have been if Harry had been her father instead of Arthur.

Very early in their wedded life together May conceived a child. Her first. She was naturally delighted but Arthur wasn't too sure. He was unemployed at the time. It was the Depression. He felt obliged by the normal expectations of society to be able to care for his wife and any offspring. Didn't he? But how could he do so when there was no work to be had?

It's not a good time to be having a child May dear!

May's mother wasn't happy by the announcement either but her reasons were different. Her's were all about scandal and saving face. The pregnancy had come too soon after the wedding she told May.

What will people think May, that you and Arthur had to get married?

It simply won't do at all May her mother said. You are a nurse. You will have to arrange to get rid of it. It's too soon to be having a child May! You can see that can't you May?

Nonono! It's my baby, you can't make me get rid of it!

Unfortunately for May, Arthur agreed with her mother. The pregnancy must be terminated. Soon. There was simply no other option.

But I want to have this baby mother and how can you go along with her Arthur? This is your child too!

But May had been trained from an early age to be the dutiful daughter and now the dutiful wife. The joy of her pregnancy turned to sadness and despair. She knew she was beaten. She knew they would win.

May agreed finally to arrange for the termination at the hospital.

She felt bitter. Betrayed by Arthur. Beaten by her mother.

The baby that she had suddenly conceived in a moment of wedded passion was to be taken away from her.

May briefly struggled with thoughts of resistance and defiance. But in the end she knew she would obey their wishes.

There there May stiff upper lip there's a good girl!

Jess very rarely got close to her mother. Even as an adult. She tried over the years but it never seemed to work out between them. Too many years of resentment. Too much damage already done.

Jess tried to discuss the early years with May. She wanted to see what had motivated her. But mostly she drew a blank. May would pull a curtain of silence down as effectively as though there was a brick wall between them. Which she supposed there was in a way.

Then one day when Jess's own children were toddlers May began to open up. She told Jess about her first pregnancy. Before James. And Hannah and Ruby and Jess. May told Jess about the circumstances surrounding the abortion. A tear rolled down May's cheek as she blurted out the briefest details. Just imagine that! What a way to start your married life together. Poor May!

Jess couldn't imagine how traumatised May must have been. What a cowardly and invasive act by the two people she trusted the most. Jess knew that she had loved that baby and wanted it dearly, but had got rid of it out of a misguided sense of loyalty and duty to her husband and mother.

Hush little baby don't you cry, moma's gonna sing you a lullaby.

Jess watches her own son blow out the candles on his birthday cake. There are seven. She envies him.

Lucky lucky lucky.

Smoke drifts up as the flames are extinguished one by one. The little boy smiles up at Jess as if to seek approval for a job well done. His sister and the other children gather round the birthday boy. Everyone sings happy birthday to him. The boy looks down, embarrassed.

The table is strewn with sausage rolls and fairy bread and party pies and hot dogs. There are small bowls of sweets and large bowls of chips and cheezels.

Each place is set with a fancy paper plate and a party hat for each guest.

Happy birthday to you, happy birthday to ....

Jess searches her adult memory bank to find the happy birthdays of her own childhood but there are none. At least if there were, you'd think that she would remember. Wouldn't you?

But she doesn't.

Perhaps May gave Jess a birthday party once and she's forgotten.

But why is that so?

Happy bithday to you ... happy birthday to ....

James was the first born son of May and Arthur. He arrived early one September morning when May was least prepared. She glanced at him through a cloud of overwhelming tiredness and pain. She barely even lifted her head. May's brief recognition of this boy child was overshadowed by the memories of the other. The child that had been unceremoniously plucked from her womb. The first.

Her mother had said too soon too soon and Arthur had agreed. But May had been lost and it still hurt.

James was a tiny scratchy child and demanded much of May. His mother. She bought him home from the hospital swaddled tightly in blankets and placed him carefully in the nursery. Arthur stayed in the background for a moment then went back to work. The new baby was May's concern. He had other duties didn't he?

James was a difficult child but May pretended he was perfect. It was expected of her after all. She was the dutiful wife and mother and daughter. Isn't that what she had always been told? So she kept the baby clean and fed and tended the house and cooked for her husband and visited her mother.

But it was difficult for May to adjust. She yearned for solace. She wanted some freedom. But there was none to be found for May.

Harold oh Harold, where are you now?

May is still busy with the packing. Arthur is at work as usual. He wasn't home much. Not then and not later. Always working, or at least that's what he told May anyway.

James is bored and house-bound for once. May says that he must stay around today in case she needs him to help her. But he doesn't help. Just hangs around the backyard fixing up his billycart.

Jess sneaks out to see what he is up to and instantly knows that she has made a mistake. James sees her from under the tree. He calls her over.

Come here Jess I've got something for you and it's fun fun fun!

There is no escape. Jess is the youngest. She must go.

See here he says, here is my new billycart and you can have the first ride won't that be fun hey?

Nononononooooooo!

Jess screams in her head but stands there and waits for James anyway. If she goes inside to tell mum she'll cop it from both of them. So she waits.

This'll be fun sis and we won't tell mum orright we'll jez take 'er down the hill o.k.?

But it's *not* o.k.! Jess knows that. It sounds frightening and dangerous and she's scared. But she doesn't show her fear or call out for she knows it will be wasted energy. Jess follows James to the road and waits.

In yer get sis go on. Look, here's how you steer it, orright? Off yer go then, wheee!

With a push at the back of the billycart James sends Jess off down the hill. He stands and watches her progress but he doesn't run after her.

He watches from the top of the hill and hopes for the best.

Jesus Mary Mother of God help me help meeeee!

Jess is going too fast and the intersection looms up ahead. Despite what James said about steering Jess cannot do it. The rope hurts her hands. Jess is going faster and faster now. She is out of control. She is going to crash at the bottom of the hill.

I am I am I know it!

Jess closes her eyes moments before the sudden lurch of the billycart throws her forwards and onto the bitumen of the road. Her head hurts instantly and Jess lets out a wail of despair. She doesn't care any more if James thinks she is a weak little baby. Jess hurts all over.

I hate you I hate you!

But James doesn't care. He thinks it's funny. He races down the hill and turns over the billycart, rescuing it from where it crashed in the road. Then he thinks to rescue his sister too, but only because he knows that mother will be angry with him because she's hurt.

There there sis you'll be right come on get up now there's a good little kid. Let's have a look at yer. You'll be just fine, o.k.? I'll git a bandaid for ya back home and we won't need to tell mum will we? Sis?

Jess drives down the Great Ocean Road in the old FJ Holden. She is singing in her head. She feels free. Jess is running away. They are both running away. Jess and her partner.

Outside it is cold and grey and threatening to rain but they don't care.

Jess should be teaching of course. The phone call came at 7.30 this morning but she said no. Bugger it. She'd already planned the day.

Bree was busy in the kitchen boiling the kettle and humming away to herself when the phone rang.

No, not available today. Sorry.

But was she really? Sorry, that is. Not on your life. Couldn't care less. Didn't give a rats about working today.

So they threw the picnic hamper in the back of the old car and tootled off down the Torquay road. Headed down the coast to Lorne to join the Fly the Flag Car Rally. Just for fun. Wheee!

Gorgeous scenery in this part of the world isn't it says Jess. Stunning really. No wonder it's such a popular tourist location.

Reminds me of the coast drive down the south island of New Zealand Jess says to Bree. Wonder if we'll see any seals?

But they don't. Instead they see lots of surfers. Small black dots bobbing about in the water waiting for the right waves to come along.

Jess watches them as they drive. Part of her wants to be out there with them in the swell of the ocean. But it is cold and overcast. It is already Autumn. Jess decides she is happy to be in the car where it is warm.

Look says Bree. There's some of the rally cars heading towards us. Look look look.

They toot and wave as some of the old cars approach. Bree breaks into a smile as she waves at the drivers and Jess laughs at her enthusiasm. It is infectious. They are both laughing now.

They arrive in Lorne and pull into a car space near the shops. There are lots of rally cars parked up and down the street. All types and colours and in excellent condition.

Look look look!

When Jess was little they didn't own a car. She didn't even know anyone who owned a car in Newcastle in those days. People must have, of course. But they weren't in her world.

Arthur and May rarely went out socialising or visiting except to see grandma and Auntie Maud. Grandma was Arthur's mother and she was bed ridden.

Aunt Maud was Arthur's sister and she lived with grandma and looked after her. Aunt M was a teacher. She never married. May called her a spinster, and that always sounded cold and hard and strange.

Jess didn't know what spinster meant but she sure didn't want to be one of those when she grew up.

Tread on a crack and you'll marry a . . . .

Perhaps that's what had happened to Aunty Maud, she'd never played the game and never had the chance to find out what would happen. Jess didn't know. She was too little then to understand such things.

But despite the fact that she never married and lived with gran till she passed on, Jess didn't think of Aunt M as being disadvantaged in any way. Quite the opposite in fact. From what Jess could see she had a comfortable life and a career and a nice warm home and lovely clothes. There were no arguments and no fights in her house. No sisters to boss *her* around, were there?

Gran may have been demanding in her own way but Aunt M was the one in control. Not like May who was at everyone's beck and call.

I'm home dear is my sherry ready where's the paper are the children bathed is tea ready are my shirts washed and by the way, how was your day dear?

May dressed for tea every night in those days. It was the done thing she said and anyway father expected it. He'd worked hard all day she said and deserved to come home to a tidy house and neat clean children and his sherry poured and his pipe ready and tea cooking on the stove.

Didn't he?

Queenie queenie who's got the ball?

So every afternoon long before the children wanted to come inside they were called in to tidy themselves up for Arthur's homecoming.

A scrub behind the ears with a flannel and a brush of hair in the bathroom then clean clothes laid out on the bed.

God I hate the fuss and ritual of Arthur's arrival each evening seethed Jess.

It all seemed so pointless and futile and selfish. Why did they have to finish outdoors to fit in with father all the time?

The older sisters of course would use this time to further exploit Jess and tell tales that usually weren't true.

Daddy daddy Jess got in trouble at school today. She did daddy, truly she did.

It wasn't true of course. Not then in the early days. Jess was quiet and bright and attentive. She learned quickly and rarely came even close to getting into trouble at school.

But Arthur wasn't to know that, he never went near the school. May didn't either for that matter. The less she had to do with us during the day the better it seemed to Jess. And that of course included anything to do with Junction East primary school.

Arthur would look over his glasses at Jess and frown through the smoke which curled up from his pipe. Silence ensued. Always silence first.

But threats hung in the air behind his chair as she stood waiting.

Waiting.

Go to your room!

No no! I didn't do anything and I didn't get into trouble at school Hannah is lying daddy. I'm a good girl. Remember?

Silence again then a cough as he turns away. Jess knows she is beaten once more and she must obey. Arthur returns to his paper in silence. He sips his sherry and puffs on his pipe.

Jess is left alone in her room behind the closed door.

It's not fair it isn't I hate you I hate you!

But it doesn't matter. Noone will come and save her. Jess is alone and she knows it. Alone with her thoughts and her words and her stories.

They will save her.

Once upon a time there was a little girl and her name was . . . .

May was surrounded by boxes. Lots of boxes. More than she could bear to look at if the truth be known.

The packing wasn't going as quickly as Arthur had hoped and of course he blamed May. She was so tired of it all. The packing and moving. Why had she agreed to it in the first place she wondered?

The sea oh the sea am I really leaving you behind?

All May's memories and life experiences belonged here in Newcastle and she was terrified suddenly at the reality of the leaving. How had it happened? That's what May wanted to know. *Had* she agreed to it or had Arthur just insisted? As always.

May didn't understand the life forces that were taking her away from her beloved Newcastle. It was all simply too much now that the departure was looming. She couldn't cope with the thought of the final farewell. So she took to her bed and shut the door on the outside world of boxes and upheaval. The household dramas and the demands of her brood would just have to take care of themselves May decided. It was all too much.

I can't go I can't! How will I cope without mother and my beautiful sea?

Jess and Bree get out of the car and stroll across to the beach. Jess digs her toes in the sand and feels the familiar gritty warmth. The sea laps at her feet and calls her once more. Just as it did when she was the little sister all those years ago in Newcastle. She closes her eyes and is transported back through time. Jess feels the wind on her face as she scrambles amid the rockpools searching for starfish. Her joy is solitary for the sisters are not there. She is alone once more in her world.

Lucky lucky me.

Lets go for coffee Bree calls. She wants to stroll over and take a closer look at the classic cars. Look look!

Jess shakes from her reverie and grabs Bree's hand as they cross the road. Her reminiscing is stilled but a smile lingers as she holds onto the picture of the small white-haired girl on the beach. It was so long ago yet sometimes the reality seems so close. A gossamer thread away.

Jess orders two lattes with a dash of cold milk and a hot cross bun and sausage roll. Let's sit outside where we can see the beach she says to Bree. I want to watch the waves.

Bree giggles at Jess in reply as she sips at the coffee. You always have to be near the sea Jess don't you says Bree.

But the roar of the waves and the dash of the sea as it curled and crashed against the sea wall was in Jess's blood wasn't it wasn't it?

Jess carries the kindling in and stacks it by the wood fire. Then she brings in some pine cones and logs and puts them in grandma's old washing basket by the fridge. Next Jess waters the plants while she plans the day in her head. She has already done the crosswords and read the news and had breakfast and showered.

Jess knows she is stalling a little this Monday morning. She puts off going in to the office but somewhere in her mind she knows that the writing is waiting.

The washing machine shudders to a halt nearby so Jess empties it and trudges out to the clothesline. The builders have arrived next door to start work on the new house but Jess doesn't watch them this morning.

I need to get on with the words. I am ready now.

The little girl ran and ran along the long stretch of beach ahead of the others. The waves splashed at her feet and the wind tugged at her hair and whipped it across her face. But she didn't care. She was happy to be here once more. The sea. Her home. She sang in her head as she ran.

Sea shells cockle bells all in a row . . . .

She wanted the others to go away and leave her alone by the shorebreak. But she knew they would not. She was too little yet.

Baby baby, you're just a baby!

Hannah and Ruby were up ahead with mother. James was nowhere to be seen. As usual. Lucky James, mother hardly ever bothered with him! Most of the time he could do as he pleased. Lucky lucky.

But Jess is too small to be trusted with doing as she pleases. She is entrusted to the care of the older girls.

Not so lucky!

Jess hears May calling to her from further along the beach but she ignores her for as long as she can. It might not be a wise thing to do but Jess is having too much fun just jumping in the shallow waves there by the shore. She is making up a story in her head where she is strong and powerful. It is a wonderful adventure. *They* are not included.

But May's voice grows louder and becomes insistent so Jess turns and runs down the beach towards them. Her family. Sisters and mother. Absent brother and father.

Come here child come here demands May as Jess draws near to the group on the sand. We have been waiting for you. We need to go. Hurry now. Hurry.

No no I want to stay here longer and play in the waves and visit the rockpools and search for crabs and lie on the sand and bury my toes.

Please mother can't we stay for a while I'll be good honest I will please!

Hannah takes hold of Jess roughly and pushes her forwards so that she almost falls.

I hate you I hate you . . .

Shut up baby and do as you're told! Hahaha!

Jess knows she is beaten once more. It is senseless to protest. She follows Hannah up the grass hill towards the path. Along to the docks. Past the ships. Across the road. Past the train station. Past the shops and the hotel. Up the hill. Past the park. Along our street.

But the beautiful words are still in her head and the sea is still with her.

Jess doesn't want to be here. Home. She silently curses them as the gate swings open and they file in. Mother and the three girls. And James, last of course.

Off to your rooms May says and get busy. We have more packing to do before daddy gets home from work tonight. I'll come and see how you are going after I've had a cup of tea. Don't disturb me now. Off you go, hurry now.

Jess doesn't understand why they are going. She doesn't want to pack up her things. It just doesn't make sense. This is her home.

Why are we leaving? Why does daddy have to start another job in another city?

Coals to Newcastle, that's what May always said. So why leave then?

But Jess was the youngest and had no say in things. Noone listened to her anyway so she didn't bother them with wasted questions. They would be drowned in silence. Jess knew.

Leave me alone child can't you see I'm having a rest ask your father when he comes home go away go away.

Jess's chest feels heavy when she wakes. She gets out of bed and gathers the towelling robe tightly around her. There are things she has to do today. Jess doesn't want to succumb to a cold. She doesn't have the time.

It was the same back then in her childhood. The colds. Lots of them. Chest and throat and ear infections. Of all the children Jess seemed to get them the most. And of course May resented Jess even more then didn't she? Despite the fact that she was a trained nurse. You'd think that would make a difference but not when it came to her family. Not with Jess anyway.

Mother mother I don't feel well. My throat hurts and my ears ache.

Shush child, May would say. Take this hot lemon drink and go back to bed. I'll come and see how you are going later. There there now stop your whining and be a brave girl. I'll bring a hot water bottle for your ear in a little while.

But it hurts it hurts!

Little Jess lay in bed with the covers pulled up tightly over her head. She wants to cry with the pain but knows it would do no good. The sisters don't care. They come in and jump on Jess's bed and tease her.

Baby baby you're just a baby!

Go away go away Jess wants to shout at them. But she knows that will make things worse so she keeps her eyes closed and hopes they will soon leave.

Jess drops off to sleep. The room is quiet when she wakes and her sisters are not there. She is alone.

Thank you thank you.

Jess gazes up at the ceiling and stretches out under the thin old blankets. She doesn't call out or make any noise for she doesn't want anyone to know she is awake. Jess wants to be alone to write stories once more in her head.

Once upon a time there was a little girl and she had two sisters and they . . .

Jess Jess get up it's time to get ready for tea and why have you been sleeping I need to get the room tidied hurry hurry!

Jess doesn't know if she's asleep or awake.

What do you want? Go away, go away.

Hannah is beside the bed now and yanks back the covers. She pulls the feverish Jess out of her bed and laughs.

Look at you Jess you are such a mess shrieks Hannah. Hurry up and make the bed and get dressed for tea or mother will be cross with you. Hurry up now, there's a good little girl! Hannah doesn't care at all that Jess is sick.

I hate you I hate you!

But Hannah has gone and Ruby comes in. She smiles at Jess but says nothing. She doesn't offer to help make the bed. Ruby rarely offers to help do anything. That's just how it is in my house.

May leans back on the heavy cedar bedhead and sighs. She feels adrift. Her world is dishevelled. May is bereft at the impending upheaval.

Her head swims with the mundane but her heart flutters with some tiny shred of hope. A tattered but bedraggled relic of something lost long ago.

A dream.

And May *had* had dreams in her past. Lots of them. Hopes and loves and needs all intertwined in her solitary moments. Away from the children and Arthur. Away from her demanding parents. And away from the house on the hill.

Ah the sea is calling to her teasing her taunting her to come to the foam and soak in the saltspray like her father and grandfather before her.

But if May had pushed the dreams far down into her subconscious they were not totally submerged. Merely banished for a while. Shoved aside and sacrificed on the altar of domestic duties. May had of course seen to that. So had Arthur with his insistence on wedded obedience.

But sometimes as May watched the little white-haired girl dance on the shoreline she remembered her own childhood. Didn't she?

Ah Jess you are too young too young to lose the joy my youngest daughter.

A pang of guilt swept through May's muddled conscience as she lay prone on the marriage bed where she and Arthur had conceived the four offspring. Poor

May was tossed this way and that as surely as if she'd been aboard her grandfather's ship the night it went down with all hands in a terrible gale. Her brain ached and her limbs became limp with the agony of it all.

It seemed to May that chunks of herself were being broken off suddenly there in the bedroom and floating out to sea with the flotsam and jetsam of the shipwreck. She was dashed on the rocks of her own mortality. Everything that had anchored May so far in this life was becoming adrift and May felt helpless to stem the advancing tide. The waters were rising. May was drowning in the seas within and she felt overwhelmed.

Take me down to the sea grandad . . . take me down to the sea.

Jess is hiding under the bed. It is dark but she does not mind. She is playing the game again by herself. Hannah and Ruby and James and mother don't know she's here. She lies very still and quiet to keep them away. Jess shuts them out of her world. Arthur is at work as usual so she doesn't include him in the game either. It is just Jess. Alone.

Small cracks of light filter through under the edge of the blanket Jess has dragged over the bed. She opens her eyes and watches the patterns of dust floating beside her. It is beautiful. Jess wishes she were a speck of dust so that she could float and drift away away. Out of the window. Down the hill. Above the docks and out to sea. Free. Jess would be free.

But she is not to be released. She is stuck here in the bedroom in the brick house. Waiting.

Oranges and lemons say the bells of St Clements . . . .

Jess shuts her eyes tight and sing songs in her head to pass the time. There is only silence. Nothing more.

She knows that soon she will be summoned and she will have to go. She will have to end the game. Mother and Hannah and Ruby will see to that. But for now Jess doesn't care. She is alone with her words and her songs.

When will you pay me say the bells of Old Bailey . . . .

Jess smiles as she sings. A warm inner smile, not the one you have to wear when daddy comes home or grandma greets you. A real smile.

Sometimes things work out in life and sometimes they don't. Maybe most of the time it's in our control and it's all about choices. But sometimes there's something else too. Fate. Luck. Whatever.

Jess knew. Believe me, she knew.

You would think that being middle-aged would bring all the usual stuff. Happiness, well-being, a comfortable living, love. For Jess it had.

Lucky lucky me.

But it wasn't always that way and Jess should know. Sometimes she thought that you had to walk to hell and back before things came together and gave you a break in life. Sometimes you needed the rough to appreciate the smooth. At least Jess did, and that's all she had to measure things by.

But when Jess was little she didn't know such things.

How could she? She was way too young.

All Jess knew as the small white-haired girl was that life seemed a never-ending series of days and nights governed by games and rules. Not Jess's rules. No, not for a long time. They were the rules Jess had to live by nonetheless.

Come here child daddy is waiting for you. Hurry up and get ready for school Jess, Hannah is waiting. You haven't done your jobs yet Jess hurry hurry. Come here go there do that sit still shush shush child! Nononono!

Rules and commands and orders. They filled Jess's childhood world and she thought that's all there was.

Except for the words.

It was many years later that Jess discovered laughter and freedom and joy and happiness and fun. She never knew those things. Did she?

Jess looks back sometimes and asks herself if there ever *was* fun in the house when she was the little sister. She supposes there must have been. But she doesn't remember.

How could she forget such an important emotion?

Jess doesn't understand how it is possible to forget happiness, so maybe there was none.

Hannah and Ruby might see things differently and Jess is sure they do. But *they* were not the little sister. Jess was.

Baby, baby!

Jess tries hard to recall those years of so long ago to search for clues. But none come. She is left vacant. Empty, like the years without love. Why would that be?

Jess flicks back through the locker of memories. Back to Newcastle. Back to the sea and the brick house on the hill.

She trawls the seas of her childhood for happy recollections but they are gone. Maybe they weren't there in the first place? She just doesn't know.

Hannah and Ruby always said she was far too serious and way too smart and maybe they were right. But that doesn't help Jess now. It only adds to her frustration in searching for answers.

May is frantic now with the packing. So much to do and time is running out. Father is insistent that the family is going to Sydney. It doesn't matter that mother will be leaving her roots. That the children will be leaving the only home they have ever known. It is work. Promotion. Opportunity. That's what Arthur tells May as they sip their sherry in the evening. It is for the best dear.

But May has had enough. She has taken to her bed and will not be interrupted. Her door is firmly closed and woe betide the children if they make a noise. So they tiptoe about the house and avoid going anywhere near May's bedroom. They know she is not to be disturbed.

But of course that means Jess is at the mercy of the two sisters for the day. She knows the rules. The games begin again.

Outside in the back garden Jess has a small cactus growing in a discarded green glass butterbox. It is sitting on a shelf by the fence. The sun dances on the crinkle-cut glass and to Jess it seems like magic. She sits still and silent and watches the light sparkle on the butterbox garden.

It is like a little world and it makes Jess feel happy for a moment in time. Jess knows it won't last, it never does. But she is happy all the same.

Once upon a time there was a fairy princess and she . . . .

Jess scans the picture of her unborn grandchild and smiles. Despite the fogginess of the ultrasound

Jess feels connected. She sticks the latest image on the fridge with bluetack. Scorpio or Libra Jess wonders?

Scorpio. Like me.

Jess marvels at the advantages of technology and contemplates how different things are now. With her two children Jess had to imagine what the unborn child was like based on drawings in numerous baby books.

Jess wonders if May ever mused much about her unborn children prior to their arrival in this world. She had five of them after all. Six if you count the aborted one. Surely she must have wondered, she was a trained nurse after all. Did the nurse part of May override the mother part and take control?

Jess doesn't know. It's too late to discover how May felt about each pregnancy as it overtook her ageing body. But Jess is curious.

Five babies. James, Hannah, Ruby, Jess and Paul. Five siblings and five full-term pregnancies.

But you were the one that nearly killed her, at least that's what she said.

Part of Jess wishes there had only been one child. Her. Not the others. They took too much of May's energy and strength and time. They took away Jess's childhood. They were there first and that was the trouble.

May had simply run out of puff by the time Jess came along.

One potato two potato three potato four . . . .

Number four. That was Jess. Too late. When she was four May was forty. Poor May. Already consumed by guilt. Overcome with a constant barrage of life-demands imposed on her each waking moment.

But May had help with each baby. Mrs C came and stayed in the brick house in Newcastle for two months with each new child. Live-in carer. Full time nanny. Substitute mother for the growing brood.

But Jess was the last to have Mrs C and of course was way too young to remember her at all. She only knew because May had told her years later.

When Jess had her own children.

Don't be silly dear I can't come up and help you why don't you hire someone like I did?

Hire someone? Use a nanny? Me? What did she think we were? Jess lived on a teacher's salary for God's sake! Paying for help was simply out of the question and Jess was foolish enough to think that families provided that sort of support for each other. Didn't they?

Five potato six potato seven potato more!

It didn't really matter. Jess muddled through motherhood in a quiet country backwater with the help of her husband and friends anyway. Despite her mother and sisters and brother who were all too far away and too busy and too everything for Jess. She was used to survival without them wasn't she?

May lies prone on the marital bed. It is dark in her room in the Newcastle house. The blinds are down. She is alone.

It is only a matter of time before Arthur will return from work and she will have to get up. But for now May stays silent and still in the middle of the bed. Not moving a muscle she tries to shut out the world. Or what's left of it anyway.

Nonono Arthur I can't leave my beloved Newcastle ... please don't ask me to do that ... pleeease!

But in her head May knows they are soon going despite what her needs are. It is not her needs that Arthur is concerned with of course but his own. It is *his* future and livelihood that are important. Not May's or the children's. They only count as accessories in Arthur's grand scheme.

But it is not her head that is causing poor May problems at the moment. It is her *heart* that aches. She feels as though somehow she is being dismembered. Torn apart. Losing her grip on the world as she knows it.

I wish I'd settled for Harry after all . . . . Harry Harry where are you?

Jess recalls the feelings of new parenthood as she contemplates becoming a grandma now. What does she remember? How did she feel? What was it like as a new mother all those years ago? Will it be the same now as grandma?

Jess knows that she shouldn't be buying stuff for the baby yet but already the toys and the baby clothes are amassing. It's such fun this grandma thing. Jess loves it.

Look oh look at that gorgeous green frog we just have to buy it yes yes!

Jess and Bree laugh at the counter of the chemist shop as they pay for the frog with wheels. They press the red dots and the frog sings a nursery rhyme.

They are having so much fun already being grandmas but the baby is still months away. Jess giggles at Bree as they leave the shop with the frog stuck between them. They are like naughty children. They go and have a coffee and tuck the frog safely under the table.

Jess's little feet are running but seem to be going nowhere. She is stuck to the pavement. It is hot and Jess is turning to glue. She cannot breathe. She is going to suffocate there out the front of the Newcastle house and noone will find her in time. Heeeeelp!

Humpty dumpty sat on a wall, humpty dumpty . . . .

Come here you silly child there you are we have been looking for you mother wants us inside to wash up for lunch, hurry hurry! The two sisters.

61

Jess cannot escape them. She knows she cannot. They will make her go inside. It doesn't matter to them. Or to May of course.

She pretends that she doesn't see. That's part of the game she plays. The adult-game. Her rules, not Jess's. Never.

Humpty dumpty had a big fall.

But in Jess's head she plays games too. She plays by her rules, not theirs. *All the King's horses and all the King's men.*

Hannah marches Jess off to the bedroom and shuts the door carefully behind. She is careful to put another barrier up. Hannah has that look about her that says don't mess with me. Jess never does. She knows better than to mess with anyone in the family. Hannah especially.

Couldn't put Humpty together again.

Jess plays games in her head. They help to keep out the dread she feels. They soothe her because sometimes she needs soothing. Most of the time in fact. Especially when she is alone with Hannah.

One potato two potato three potato four.

There *are* four. Children. Jess's family. And Jess is number four.

Of course.

Baby baby baaaby!

But Jess is not a baby any more and she knows it. *They* know it too but they continue to treat her like one. Sometimes more than others.

The two sisters.

Put her in the pram with dolly's bonnet on again Ruby and we'll take her down the street and pretend she's deformed hahahaha!

And they did. Often. When mother was having one of her turns in the bedroom.

I'll push her says Hannah, it was my idea.

Off they go out the gate and down the hill. Ha ha ha. Isn't this funny Ruby what do you think shouts Hannah? Doesn't Jess look cute all squashed in there with the bunny rug pulled up tight over her? I'll bet people will give us some money for her if we ask.

And they did of course. Threepence here and there. For the poor little urchin in the pram. What a shame they all said. Such a cute little thing isn't she? There there dear.

Isn't that great say Hannah and Ruby as they run away laughing. Jess is left stranded in the pram.

Hahaha.

Hannah and Ruby would soon return with bags of lollies from the corner store bought with the proceeds of deception. But Jess never got any.

Of course.

The two older sisters would scoff down the sweets before pushing the pram back home. Jess would be ordered out before they reached the house. They knew there'd be trouble if May caught them but of course she never did. She didn't care. May was too busy surviving her own demons to worry about Jess.

Five potato six potato seven potato more.

And May *did* have five in the end of course. Children, that is. Not potatoes. And thank heaven for whatever means of birth control she used that there weren't more of us thinks Jess. May barely coped as it was. And of course Arthur was little help when it came to the raising of the brood he'd helped produce. Too busy at work wasn't he?

Or that's what he told May at least but Jess often wondered?

Arthur's just like Picasso, May used to say with a giggle to anyone who'd listen. Though of course Jess never knew what she meant then.

Not till years later. Jess didn't understand that May was talking about Arthur and his sexual prowess.

But even poor May didn't suspect that Arthur had a secret . . . did she?

May never told Jess any of those things when she lived in the brick house on the hill in Newcastle. Jess was the baby after all.

Too young to understand.

But not too young to feel the early seeds of discord in this strange family that claimed her was she?

May wakes suddenly from her restlessness. She feels fretful and agitated. As though she should be somewhere else and not here in the darkened bedroom.

What is happening to me?

May covers her eyes for the briefest of moments in a vain attempt to delay the getting up. But she knows it is late in the afternoon and soon Arthur will be home from the office. Everything is out of kilter in her life. She is bereft.

Why are we going and how will I cope?

May's sense of duty overrides her anxiety and she forces herself up off the bed. It is time to resume the mantle of mother and wife once more. She knows that. It is what she is.

But it's not who she is . . . . is it?

Jess and Bree are on the plane to the USA. It is dark outside. Jess feels stuck in some sort of timewarp. It is weird.

Bree sits beside her watching a second in-flight movie. Jess does another crossword then puts on the headphones to chill out with some music. Her feet and legs bob to the rhythm as she tries to keep the circulation going in the cramped conditions. It's a long flight and Jess feels powerless.

I want to get out and walk by the water.

Instead Jess shuts her eyes and dreams.

Suddenly it seems they are on the descent into Los Angeles.

Whoa, what's happening here?

Passengers are shuffling in their seats as the cabin crew prepare for landing. The captain makes an announcement over the speakers.

Outside Jess glimpses the rush of trees and grass and roads and houses and traffic as the speeding plane drops closer to the runway.

It always looks the same. Perth, Sydney, New York, London, Brisbane, Hobart, Detroit, Auckland, Paris. Houses, roads, offices, grass, trees, shops, cars, motorways. A kaleidoscope of images. It's like a silent movie spinning on fast forward. Bizarre.

Jess turns to Bree as the seat belt light flashes off. They smile at each other in anticipation and with subdued excitement. They are like kids. Conspiritorial and giggly. Silly really, they are both middle-aged.

But what the heck.

Look look Jess cries as she grabs luggage from the overhead locker. *We're here, we're here.*

LAX airport is sure busier than Tullamarine yells Bree above the din. So many people. Rush rush rush!

Jess grabs Bree's hand and they follow the masses, trying to keep some of the people from their flight in view. The monitors show where to go. Customs, strange voices, crowds, elevators, passports, sniffer dogs, x-rays, noises. They love it despite the confusion. It's so in-your-face and so refreshing after being cooped up in the aircraft.

We're here, we're here!

Jess sits on her unmade bed in the brick house on the hill. It is the day they are moving. Still Jess doesn't understand what is happening.

How can we go and live somewhere else? This is my home.

It's all Jess knows. It's where she was born, her whole world.

But May says they are leaving today. The packing is almost complete save for a few last-minute items. Soon the truck will be here to collect everything for the journey to Sydney. The children are nervous and irritable. Jess hates being in the house now.

Mother mother can we go down to the beach one more time?

Jess wants to feel the freedom once more. She wants to run along the shore and splash in the waves. But how can she say goodbye to her beloved rockpool?

But of course May says no. Don't be so silly Jess what are you thinking the taxi will soon be here to take us to the station to catch the train.

Come here child and stop that nonsense we have to go. Brush your hair and sit still and woe betide you if you crumple your dress before we leave. Hannah look after your sister will you while I go and pack the last few things.

Nonono, I'll be fine by myself. I don't want Hannah to take care of me mother, I will just sit here quietly, I will I will.

Jess draws in her breath and waits patiently for Hannah. But she is in luck. Hannah is busy in the bathroom and doesn't hear.

Thankyou thankyou thankyou!

Jess wants to cry because she feels so alone and so sad at the upheaval. But she doesn't protest. Instead Jess sits quietly and waits. But she is crying inside at the realisation that this is an ending somehow. Jess doesn't really know what is ending but she knows it is *something*. Something that she can't put it into words in her head.

Something inside me feels hard and a part of me is turning to stone.

Jess feels as though it is somehow her fault. What has she done to make the world change so suddenly?

The Grand old Duke of York, he had ten thousand men, he marched them up to the top of the hill . . . .

It is grey and bleak outside. Jess feels as lost as the sunshine. Her office is cluttered and her brain is the same on this Monday morning in May. Winter is almost here and somehow that unsettles her.

Jess is fidgety and jittery.

The printer beside her spits out hard copies of the words and Jess scans them haphazardly to check for typo's. But her heart isn't in it this morning. She is thinking of other things. Family, friends, food.

Jess wants the words back so that she can get on with the writing task.

Then he marched them down again.

Images and songs come back to Jess from her childhood as she gazes through the stained glass window. What is it about this time of year that haunts her? Why does she feel adrift?

Jess doesn't really mind the colder season. Not after all those years in the north east with frost and snow and stoking the wood fires.

Jess is suddenly back there when her children were little. Back to the small country town. Back where they had big dogs and chooks and guinea pigs for pets. Back in the river valley surrounded by mountains.

The lake and the cold winter walks in the frost with boots crunching on white as the dogs ran ahead with steamy breath. Jess's breath curled too in the fog as she called out to the dogs. Come back come back here!

They ran down the slope near the oval and past the school, then on along the track to the lake. Most times it was grey and still with mist rising in the early morning dew. But they didn't care, the dogs and Jess. They revelled in the quietness and the stillness and the natural beauty.

Back home the children would be stirring and Jess hurried to get the fire going to warm up the place before school. Small droplets of water would run down the insides of the bedroom windows on those cold nights when they tucked themselves deep under the doonas to keep warm.

Jess didn't heat the bedrooms then, only the living area. But the house was small so it didn't seem to matter too much. It held the cosiness.

May and the four children were on the train to Sydney before she realised where they were. What had happened? May was puzzled and anxious as the rapidly-moving world spun in her head. It was frightening. May didn't like it one bit and she caught her breath before the feeling of complete abandonment overcame her. What should she do now she wondered? Was there anyone at all to save her?

May closed her eyes and clenched her fists against the tempest, but it brought only temporary relief. She felt like her world had disappeared to be replaced by the unknown. She was drowning in her own doubts, scared and alone. Where was Arthur when she most needed him?

Jess was reminiscing about her adult life. Her mind was stuck back in the country when she was a young mother. She smiled at the simple joys they had all shared living in the small weatherboard house near the lake.

In winter they would all go skiing. It was such fun. The children started when they were toddlers on borrowed skis. Jess and her husband used to take them up the chair in their laps and ski down with them between their skis. It wasn't long of course before the two children were proficient skiers and could handle almost every run on the mountain.

May and her brood are in the new house in Sydney. Jess is lonely but she doesn't miss people. What she misses is her beach and the sea and the rockpools. She longs for the walks downtown and the climb up the hill and King Edward Park and the

Obelisk. Jess doesn't miss school except for the books and story time.

But she still has her world of words, so at least she has brought something of importance to the new house.

When Jess stands at the window of the sunroom in the new house she can see the sea. It's not the same as her Newcastle sea though. There are more waves here and an island called Wedding Cake. Jess thinks that's an odd name for an island, but her mother tells her it's because it looks like a wedding cake when the sea is rough and surrounded by frothy waves.

On weekends sometimes they have surf races around the island in the surfboats and if Jess looks very carefully she can make out the men rowing. When it's rough they often capsize and the crew have to scramble back on board and get rowing again. Jess doesn't understand why they would do this, it seems silly.

On her first day at the new school Jess is given a note about collecting rags for charity. Jess isn't sure why people need rags to make money, but she tells the teacher they don't have any at home. This is because mother has used them all to stop the rain coming in the windows.

They leaked on the first night in the new house, and daddy said he'd get them fixed as soon as he could find a reliable tradesman. Jess knew that mother didn't believe him though, she knew he'd forget. Arthur's mind was always on work in those days, and the running of the family and household was pretty well all left to May.

It is cold and frosty this morning and when Jess emerges from the house her breath steams in the air. She is rugged up in a winter jacket and hat and gloves for the early morning walk with the dog. Mack bounds around her feet and jumps ahead as Jess fastens his lead. He is frisky as ever as they head out the gate and up the road. Mack pulls on his lead. He sniffs and growls and roves back and forth across the dewy grass as they pass houses still clothed in silent wet darkness. Occasional car lights flash past and Mack barks and leaps at them as though they are somehow a threat.

Jess laughs at his antics and revels in the joy of once more walking in the cold mornings. Hints of frost lie spread before them as they walk, reminding Jess of the countless country walks of her past.

She pulls the warm beanie further down over her ears and smiles to herself. The suburban neighbourhood has become familiar to her now.

It feels like she has finally come home despite the difference to other places Jess has lived.

Jess is nine years old. They have lived in the sprawling brick house in Coogee now for two years. Jess is taller and older and more independent than when she left Newcastle but still May insists that her sisters take care of her most of the time. Jess knows that they resent having to do it and she still has to play by their rules. But at least they don't call her *baby* any more.

The three sisters have been out playing up the road from their house in Coogee. Tiggy is what they are playing and of course Hannah is the boss. As usual.

Jess is running down the street to find a place to hide. She jumps up and runs along a low brick wall. Just for fun. To be different. But Hannah calls out suddenly and Jess is momentarily distracted. She turns to see where she is and loses her footing on the narrow bricks. Her body is propelled downwards and Jess reaches out with her hands to stop the fall. But it is too late. She hits the concrete path heavily and falls on her arm.

Owwww, she cries. Ouch, it hurts!

Hannah comes sauntering over to where Jess lies in a muddle on the footpath and orders her to sit up.

She takes a look at the tear-stained face and sneers at Jess in disgust. Jess waits for her to call out *baby baby* but instead Hannah turns away and calls out to Ruby. Come here and take a look at her arm will you sis? Does it look alright to you?

Jess doesn't know why Hannah asks Ruby's advice, she never asks anyone for help at home. Jess's arm looks a little wobbly and she's scared it's broken, but the older sisters are convinced she's just faking.

Sookie-bub says Hannah. Get up get up there's nothing wrong with you. Ruby smiles at Jess with a hint of sympathy, but she doesn't have any influence at all over Hannah and she knows it.

Come on sis, you'll be o.k.

But I'm not o.k. and I don't want to keep playing their games thinks Jess. Despite what Hannah says.

Jess howls a bleak protest at Hannah but knows she will not listen. She wipes her face and holds back the increasing pain and the tears to avoid further scorn from Hannah. Jess wants to get away somehow and run home to mother but she has to wait till the next game of tiggy begins.

And when they were up they were up, and when they were down they were down . . . .

Back home finally Jess shows May her arm and she says what were you doing child this arm looks as though it might be broken! May summons Hannah to the kitchen and demands an explanation. What on earth were you thinking Hannah can't you see that your sister is in pain?

For once it is Hannah who is in the bad books and Jess turns away and allows herself a grin of satisfaction despite the pain.

Hurry up now Hannah and get Ruby ready, we have to take your little sister to the hospital.

May puts a splint of cardboard and bandage on Jess's arm and they trudge down the street to see a doctor at the hospital. Jess is still in pain but at least has the satisfaction of knowing that she was right this time and Hannah was wrong.

And when they were up they were up.

The doctor takes x-rays and says yes yes May it's a greenstick fracture and we will have to put a cast on the child's arm. She'll have to have a small operation but it will be fine May and you're a nurse so you should know all about it shouldn't you?

But it must be different when it's your own child and May is looking a bit ruffled now with the whole procedure. As though somehow it might be her fault for not being with the child when it happened. She worries more about what Arthur will say when he gets home from work than what the child is going through.

Jess is put in a hospital gown in a hospital bed. It is all white and there are strange sounds and smells and she is frightened. But May says be a brave girl there there dear it will all be over soon.

Jess doesn't understand what is happening as she is wheeled away down a long cold corridor. Away from her mother and sisters.

Suddenly she is in a room with a large light turned on above her. It is cold and silent save for the metallic sounds of the instruments and the strange voices of nurses. Jess hears the sound of liquid being poured somewhere beside her but she doesn't understand what is happening. She tries to turn round and call out but someone is putting a mask over her face. It is soaked in something that smells disgusting.

Jess feels trapped in a cage. She is sick and woozy and the smell is so strong. She cannot escape.

I am drowning in ether and it is getting darker and darker.

I am being sucked out by the tide and I cannot reach the shore for I am growing weaker and weaker. Heeeeelp!

Time passes and suddenly Jess is awake. She feels terrible. Her whole body seems to belong to someone else and she can feel something heavy encasing her sore arm. Jess's stomach is turning cartwheels as she leans over and vomits into a silver dish being held by the nurse. She vomits and vomits. It feels disgusting. Jess sees a stream of spittle and yellow-brown fluid swimming in the bottom of the dish. She feels worse than before and can't seem to stop vomiting.

May finally appears at her bedside and reaches down to pat Jess's head briefly.

It's me she says, I'm here dear and you are going to be alright.

But Jess doesn't *feel* alright and she thinks that it's just talk. She turns away from May and faces the wall. Jess wants to sleep and get rid of all this. She wants it to go away.

Have you ever noticed that life seems to chug along in fits and starts until something major happens? Jess was in a reflective mood this wintry Monday morning.

Maybe for some people it's only minor issues that clog up the cisterns of their day to day living. Perhaps disaster never strikes most people, thought Jess. But she believed that's not true. How could it be when her own life had been full of them?

Take Jess's arrival on this planet for example. A disaster for all concerned. Well, May mainly. Arthur wasn't there of course, he never was. Five kids in all, you'd think he'd show some interest in the birthing process wouldn't you? But to give him his dues, it was hardly 'done' in those days for a father to be present at their child's delivery. And Jess guessed even if it was Arthur still wouldn't have fronted.

There would have been the inevitable excuse of course. I'm too busy today dear I have to work or do the garden or sit and smoke my pipe or read the daily paper no I can't possibly come with you darling besides what will the other children do while you're there?

And of course May wouldn't argue with him. Oh no, that wasn't done. Soldier on May stiff upper lip there there dear he is a good husband and provider after all and don't you just know it!

But poor May didn't feel at all benevolent with Jess's impending birth, which she always said was the toughest. It nearly killed me it did, she'd tell anyone and everyone afterwards. That girl was the hardest baby yet.

So right from the start Jess was somehow guilty of almost causing a huge disaster in May's life. Or near death, as she put it.

But it didn't come to that thankfully and after the initial trauma of Jess's arrival things soon began to settle down. Not that she believed May ever forgave her completely.

Jess carried that burden for most of her childhood and maybe even later too. It's not an easy thing to shake off after all.

You know she almost killed me that one ha ha ha.

Jess had to fight disaster right from the cradle and it seemed welded in her fabric somehow right from the word go. Even as she bawled through infancy. Something heavy and unknown always seemed about to engulf Jess, but she didn't know what it was. Jess didn't have the words then to say it out loud. She only knew that she was different to the others and nothing would ever really fix it as long as she was the baby.

And of course Jess *was* the baby then. Nothing could change that.

Sometimes miracles occur and sometimes they don't. Sometimes even when you believe that a miracle will save you from something nothing happens. At least not when you expect it to. That's what Jess thought as a child anyway.

But not long after her broken arm something *did* happen in Jess's world.

Just when everything had settled back to some vague form of normality in the Coogee house at the top of the path with one hundred and seven steps, it happened. A miracle. Just like that.

One night after tea Jess was sitting on the back steps looking out over Wedding Cake island. The sea was calmer than usual and the sun was going down on a hot November night. The air was sticky with the neighbourhood smells of cooking and sweat and frangipani and rotting rubbish and bare dirt. Jess could just smell the faintest waft of the ocean, but it wasn't like the saltspray of her Newcastle beach.

Jess still remembered exactly what that was like. This was different.

Arthur and May were sitting on the back verandah talking in low muffled voices but Jess could make out exactly what they were saying. Years spent listening instead of protesting had honed her skills at eavesdropping. Jess sat still in the shadows and waited for their conversation to continue, wanting to hear every word.

Baby! Did he say baby? What? Who?

Jess sucked in her breath and folded further into the shadow by the stairs. Noone could see her. She strained to hear every word her parents are saying, wanting to know more about this baby they are discussing.

But May dear how can we have another baby now when I have the chance for another promotion and it might mean another move for the family soon and are you sure you are pregnant dear? When does the doctor think the baby will be due?

Baby. Mother. Pregnant. What?

Jess sits still for what seems like forever as she tries to absorb this latest news. She doesn't know much about childbirth or pregnancy yet, but she knows what she has heard and understands that she will have another brother or sister.

A baby! Wow!

Jess is back in her office. The round clock under grandfather's photo ticks loudly and she glances up to check on the time. Her grandfather stares down at her from the red frame. He is in Army uniform.

The photo is sepia and his face is stern. He looks so young but Jess knows that he is in his mid thirties in the photo. Arthur's father John. They called him Jack. Funny that. He fought in the first world war in France and Gallipoli.

Wounded twice. Repatriated to England where he was born. But he fought as an Anzac because he'd been in Australia looking for work when war broke out, so after the war the whole family emigrated.

Strange the paths life takes us on Jess thinks.

Jack was nearly forty at the end of the war and Arthur was only nine. They came out by boat of course, the four of them. Jack and Celia, Maud and Arthur. Jess never met her grandfather because he died before she was born. Another disaster, that's for sure. They said it was the effects of the mustard gas he got in the war but Jess doesn't really know. He was only fifty four poor bugger. That's younger than Jess is now.

Bloody disaster alright.

Makes you think about wars doesn't it thought Jess? She has his medals now and is bloody proud despite the fact that she never knew him.

Some people say that life is like a tapestry but Jess reckons it's more like knitting. Sometimes for no reason you just drop a stitch and the whole row disappears. Maybe if things get too bad you have to start all over again. At least that's what Jess discovered with life anyway. It's all about stops and starts and what's in between that counts. The finished thing doesn't even matter, not to Jess at any rate.

How do we know when we've finished anyway?

Disasters and magic and endurance and imagination. And lots of in betweens. That's my life Jess figures but I'm not one to complain. It's been a privilege so far.

Perhaps life is about the journey, but Jess had embarked on so many different paths. Somehow she felt like she'd lost the sequence. Dropped too many stitches along the way so that the knitting was rather haphazard.

Sometimes Jess's life was plain sailing and sometimes not but at least she'd learned to tell the difference and that's something after all.

Her sister Hannah though, now there's a different story!

Even after all the years apart and all the hurt and anguish Jess just didn't know. She couldn't work her out completely. Couldn't figure out where she inherited her bossiness and total control streak from.

It had Jess beat, but then she no longer cared.

Jess's heart tells her to let it go and get on with living her own life. *Enough is enough and it's time to move on.*

Jess is sitting on the back step of the Coogee house looking out over the sea. She wants to go down to the beach but mother wants her to stay home. The new baby has arrived and finally Jess is no longer the little one. The baby of the family. It is a small miracle, that's what she thinks.

His name is Paul and he is dark and robust and healthy. Mother smothers him in love and kisses and even father smiles at him despite his earlier misgivings. Baby Paul has suddenly become the centre of the household but Jess is not jealous. She loves him too, more than she ever thought possible. He is her salvation. Her epicentre. A new distraction in the family.

Jess is freed by Paul's arrival in the world. She feels real happiness for the first time she can remember. Jess begins to understand about emotion.

She doesn't claim him aloud as hers but in her heart she forms attachment to this new being. Her little brother.

Jess watches and waits and seizes any opportunity to care for him and protect him from the sisters. James is not interested anyway, he is far too old for babies and their messy world. He is a teenager now and has his own mysterious world to attend to.

Hasn't he always been set apart from us anyway?

But with Paul it is different. He will be mother's last child and she knows it. She is forty four years old and Paul came as somewhat of a surprise to her. A menopause baby she called it. Jess didn't know what that meant but she was happy with whatever had caused the birth. It didn't matter to her how it had happened.

Only that it *had*.

May gradually lets Jess change his nappies and feed him and burp him.

As Paul got older Jess was allowed to sit outside with him while he lay on the rug in the sunshine. She took him for short walks up the street, pushing him in the old cane pram that the mean sisters had shoved her into when they lived in Newcastle. It was freshly painted white for Paul and Jess was so proud of him as she pushed him along the pavement. He was such a special kid.

May woke one morning with the sun streaming in through the curtains. She felt refreshed and invigorated for the first time since baby Paul's arrival. Something huge had shifted in her world and touched her in the dark of the night. May was aware suddenly of her surroundings in the Coogee house. It all seemed crystal clear.

Paul by this time was almost a year old and May had turned forty five at her last birthday.

Maybe that was it, the reason for the clarity.

May sat up in the marital bed and saw things afresh. She surveyed the walls around her and decided then and there that they needed a fresh coat of paint. May got out of bed and went through to the children's room. That looked shabby too May observed.

She decided that after the older children had left for school and she'd fed Paul and cleaned up the house she would put him in the pram and go down to the hardware shop. She wanted to get some paint brochures and color charts to browse through. She felt ready to tackle the house finally. Surely Arthur would agree to some fresh paint around the place, wouldn't he?

Everything had settled down to a pattern of sorts in Coogee, but not for long. One day at dinner father announced suddenly that the family would be moving again. Going south this time. Down to Victoria. Away from the beach and Wedding Cake island.

Away from the sea baths and the steep path with so many steps to the beach. Away from the days spent lazing in the sun and fossicking for bottles to cash in for lunch. Away from the swims out to the reef through the waves of Coogee beach. And away from the few friends Jess had made in the neighbourhood which had become their home.

It will be good for me dear said father at tea. It's a promotion to a new business management school and they want me to start right away.

Weeks later mother is fussing round the kitchen after breakfast. It is the day before father is leaving and she has decided to organise a photographer to take family pictures. She has a purpose and woe betide anyone who gets in her way now!

Come here Jess and look after Paul for me while he finishes his mash. I need to talk to your father for a little while. Hurry now and be careful will you.

Mother yells out to the rest of the family as she leaves the kitchen, but it is already too late for Ruby and James. They have wandered off and Hannah is sulking again in her bedroom. Noone knows why. It's what she does now. Sulks and flounces and argues. Usually they try to tiptoe around her to avoid confrontation, but this morning May will have none of it. She puts on a rare show of defiance and marches in to Hannah's room to give commands for once.

Jess is almost out of earshot but she hears Hannah's protestations anyway. She smiles at Paul and giggles as though they are conspirators against Hannah there in the Denning Street kitchen. Paul gurgles and waves his arms to be picked up. Jess gets him out of the high chair for a cuddle. She buries her face in his messy softness.

May rushes back into the kitchen. Hurry now Jess and go and clean Paul up, the photographer will be here soon and we all need to be ready.

Hurry now there's a good girl and have you seen Ruby?

But Jess doesn't know where Ruby is this morning any more than most mornings. Ruby's not the sort of person who hangs around and makes her presence felt in the family. Not like Hannah.

Ruby is different, and maybe it's because of Hannah. Jess never thinks about it much.

Not then, anyway.

But mother is fretting and starting to work herself up to one of her moods.

Jess has seen it all before.

There is nothing she can do of course. It's not Jess's fault that Ruby is missing and Hannah is sulking in her room and James of course is nowhere to be seen. That's normal for this household, but Jess doesn't tell May that. She doesn't see things the same way. She's the mother after all and supposed to have some of the responsibility for how things run.

At least when Arthur isn't around anyway, and that's most of the time.

But that doesn't help May now, it only serves to add to her frustration. Time is fast ticking away and she feels more anxious with each passing minute.

Jess will you finish cleaning up here in the kitchen while I change the baby and get myself changed and cleaned up ready for the photos? Hurry up now there's a good girl.

Jess does as May asks because she see the signs of what lies ahead if she doesn't. She knows the anger is building. May will take to her bed behind closed doors before the day is out.

Harold why did you leave me? Haa ... rold .... !

Arthur is home. He should help his wife with the children but he doesn't. Maybe having him here today is making things worse for May. But it was her choice to do this family photo shoot so perhaps that's his excuse.

Hannah have you seen Ruby and do you know if James is out in the backyard? Go and check for me there's a good girl, calls out May from the bathroom where she is washing the baby.

Hannah slams out of the bedroom and clumps up the hallway with heavy tread. She likes theatrics, does Hannah. It's part of the power thing with her.

Look at me look at me!

But noone takes any notice this morning. Everyone is busy trying to get changed and find Ruby and be on their best behaviour for once.

The doorbell rings and suddenly the photographer is greeting May and shaking Arthur's hand and asking where they want him to set up for the photos.

He checks the light in the lounge room and says this will be just fine. Now where are all the children and how many photos do you want?

James has slunk inside and flicked a comb through his thick unruly hair so the family is almost complete. Except for Ruby. Disaster again!

Then all of a sudden the back door bangs and an unsuspecting Ruby appears in the doorway wet from a morning swim at the beach.

She grins at the family group nervously and asks what we are all doing dressed ready for church when it is only Tuesday? May sucks in her breath so as not to make a scene in front of the photographer and for once Arthur takes over. He is starting to grow bored with the whole rigmarole and wonders why he agreed to it in the first place. Probably to appease May after the upset of yet another family re-location. Maybe the guilt just got to him a little, though he would never admit it of course.

Where have you been child he barks angrily at Ruby? We have all been waiting for you to have our pictures taken now hurry up child and get dressed and for goodness sake do something with your hair.

It would never occur to Arthur to actually help. He is the head of the house. He has all the privileges. He is the breadwinner and that affords him rights, doesn't it?

May is now waiting impatiently with the baby balanced on her hip. She is trying to get the family seated firmly on the sofa while they wait for Ruby to appear. Her frustration at the delay in proceedings is evident and a storm is brewing. May has that look of *woebetide you!*

Jess knows what that means. After the photographer is gone and Arthur goes back to work. When the house is back to *normal.*

Don't shut the door again mother and leave me with them.

The family are finally ready for the photos. The children paste on artificial smiles and clasp their hands neatly in front of them.

They stare at the camera wide-eyed. First the whole family. Then the girls. Then James holding Paul. Then Arthur and May. Then each of the girls separately then James last.

It is finally done.

Sometimes life is all about taking risks. They can be calculated or not but mostly they just leap out at us unexpectedly. We either grab them and go with it or turn away and take the easy path. It's all about choice really.

Jess should know.

She had made good and bad choices over the years, but always faced up to the consequences. The same with risks. Jess had taken enough to know. Mostly they were part of her adventurous streak.

Perhaps that's all been about overcoming the barren childhood.

There are big risks and small risks but we don't see it at the time. Usually we just jump in head first and hope to goodness that we come out the other side o.k. Jess realised. The end results have probably got more to do with good luck than good management. At least that what Jess felt.

Over the years she'd jumped in the bogey hole on full tide, swum way too far in many seas, leapt into freezing rivers, canoed down rapids, galloped horses over rough terrain, climbed Mt Bogong many times, skiied to the top of Mt Kosiusko, ridden her bike flat out down mountain roads in the early morning, skiied fast down black runs, flown in a helicopter, ridden in jetboats and travelled in many countries.

But they were physical challenges that had stretched the boundaries. It was the other risks that had thrown up different consequences.

They weren't about adventure or the rush of adrenalin. They were about health and the consequences were not so immediate. Jess wished in a way they had been for she might have made different choices along the way.

Jess is ten years old. Mother says she can go to the beach with the sisters but they must stay together and be home for lunch. Jess knows that Hannah and Ruby will leave her alone to fend for herself once they are out of sight of the house, but that's o.k.

That's more than alright, it's perfect!

Jess is no longer the baby and May has other things to occupy her now. What with the baby and the imminent move down to Melbourne she is totally engrossed these days with domestic matters. And that sure doesn't involve Jess, who is free for a little while.

She bounds down the steps to the beach ahead of the others with the joy of anticipation, eager to reach her beloved sea once more.

She sells sea shells down by the shore.

James has gone out early and is nowhere to be seen. Of course. Sometimes Jess thinks he is like the invisible man.

Even when he is home for meals he hardly ever says much and who could blame him? Father argues with him most of the time anyway so it is easier for James to remain silent. Jess can understand that, she sure can!

Sometimes Jess wonders if James has stories in his head like she does? She doesn't ask him though because that would be giving away her most treasured secret. She could never do that!

Jess never wonders about the bossy Hannah or the flighty Ruby though. *They* couldn't possibly have dreams and imaginings could they?

It is still early when the three sisters arrive at the beach and Hannah runs off without even so much as a backward glance.

I don't care, it suits me fine thinks Jess.

Ruby waits around for a bit though. Where do you want to put your towel sis? Are you going in the water straight away? Do you want me to swim out to the reef with you this morning?

Jess doesn't understand this sudden interest in her welfare. It is ten years too late, but she doesn't tell Ruby that. The less she knows the better. Besides Jess knows that Ruby doesn't really care, it's all just show.

Ruby tells people what she thinks they want to hear then goes her own way anyway. All front and no substance she is. Jess has always known that.

No it's o.k. Ruby I'll be fine, you go off and meet your friends if you want to Jess replies. I'll meet you back here later and we can go home for lunch. See you.

Ruby takes another quick glance in Jess's direction then spots some of her friends further along the beach. Without another thought she runs off up the beach. Jess is alone at last. Yipee!

She places her folded towel carefully on the sand near the lifeguard's seat where she'll be able to easily find it after her swim. Then Jess races across the sand and plunges into the waves. The water claims her once more as she splashes around confidently in the blue-green world.

I am home again.

Noone has taught Jess to swim but she can do it anyway. She is strong for her age and can easily swim out to the reef. It is not very far but it is over her head. Jess doesn't mind the deep water. There are so many different colours and sights and sounds out there.

She floats on her back and lets the sun soak in. Stories and adventures form in her head as she lifts and falls gently with the waves. There are only a few swimmers out at the reef this morning but Jess doesn't care. It's soothing.

Once there was a beautiful mermaid and she . . . .

Suddenly she hears splashing and the shark alarm blares out from the beach.

Another disaster!

Jess turns and looks toward shore as she treads water. People are waving frantically from the beach. Come in come in they are yelling. Hurry hurry!

Jess swims as fast as she can towards the beach. Thankfully she can't see the shark but she swims flat out anyway. Away away. Faster and faster she goes.

Jess is like a splashing machine as she races madly through the foam. In the back of her head somewhere she knows this thrashing probably attracts sharks but she cannot stop. The water is suddenly her enemy and her worst nightmare rolled into one and she is terrified.

Once upon a time there was a little girl who got eaten by a huge shark and there was blood everywhere and she . . . .

Finally Jess is there at the shore and she throws herself down on the wet sand. Hannah and Ruby are searching in the crowd for Jess as she waves weakly at them.

I am here, I am here!

The two older sisters come running guiltily over the sand to claim Jess but they don't say much except are you o.k. sis? I'm fine Jess tells them. *But inside her head she is screaming where is the shark?*

The lifesavers launch the patrol boat and row out to where the shark was last seen. They usually go out to try to chase them away from the swimmers. Sometimes the shark is caught and dragged into shore and dumped on the beach for all to see. There is always a crowd of excited sightseers to pore over the remains on these occasion and Jess is always fascinated yet horrified. Shark stories and sightings become some of the stitches of the knitting that is Jess's life but she doesn't know that then. She is just an observer like everyone else.

Mack howls outside Jess's office window at the latest disturbance outside in the street. They are building town houses next door. The trucks and tradie's vehicles have become a constant part of Jess's daily life but she doesn't mind. It's part of living in the suburbs.

Jess and Mack walk up the road to the shops for a morning coffee. It's not too far. Flat, busy road. Buses and traffic hum beside them. Mack strains on his lead. Traffic lights halt them at the corner. Woman and dog wait patiently.

The noise of people and cars and trucks and occasional sirens suddenly seems louder. Jess waits for the green light to cross.

That's how it seems to have been for much of my life she suddenly thinks. Waiting for green lights. Stop go wait. Stall for time. Look left look right do not pass go. Maybe that's how it is with most people Jess thinks.

But most people aren't me so I can't tell how they get through Jess realises.

I only know how I got through and it sure as hell wasn't due to family. I used to wish it was but then I stopped and just got on with things.

It suddenly occurred to Jess that she had stopped standing at the yellow light and watching the red light telling her no. She gave *herself* the signal. *Green. Go.*

Looking back over the years Jess had figured out most of the paths she'd trekked. She tried not to think about it too much.

You get one shot at living on the planet and make the most of it I figure. Besides, Jess had enough silence and guilt and coldness and rejection when she was young to last a lifetime.

And enough disasters along the way too.

The three sisters trudge home up the hill in the mid-day heat in silence. Even Hannah is not being her usual bossy self. Perhaps the shark scare had an impact on her too. What if it had taken her little sister away?

Nononono!

But Ruby and Hannah are going too fast up the steps and Jess struggles to keep up.

Wait for me wait for me . . . .

Jess calls out to them and they stop. Ruby turns around and smiles at her calmly. It's o.k. sis, you'll be right. Don't tell mum about the shark or she'll be mad at us for going too far out, alright?

Jess tells them that she won't say anything but it doesn't really *feel* alright. Something is niggling at her deep down. Something a little bit scary and Jess doesn't want to think about it at all. But she knows what it is as she silently follow her sisters along Denning St.

It is the shark.

Once upon a time there was a little girl and she swam out to the reef all by herself and suddenly there was a thrashing of blood in the water and she . . .

The shark and the deep water and the sound of the siren and the anxious look on Ruby's face and the crowd on the beach and the sense of panic momentarily overcame Jess. She is only ten years old. It could have been worse, she knows that.

Much worse. Disaster!

Every action has a consequence, but usually we choose to ignore it.

When Jess was the little sister all those years ago she learned very quickly about consequences.

And games. And false hopes and promises.

Her training ground was the brick home on the hill where the people who called themselves her family lived. Jess knew they were her biological family and that they were all related but still never felt as though she belonged. And that sure had consequences.

Take last week for example when Jess had unexpectaedly bumped into her brother-in-law. The one who sent the email.

Him.

It was as though she'd seen a stranger. Jess couldn't fathom who he was till the last second as they passed outside the hospital.

Who are you she thought as he neared, do I know you? I think I've seen you somewhere before!

He's been married to Hannah for forty years. You should know him, poor bugger! What a life! He can have it.

Come here darling get ready darling phone your mother darling no not those ones dear have you forgotten we're going out darling?

Aaaagh!

Jess switches her brain away from Hannah and tries to focus on why she is here at the hospital. It is Bree who shares her life now. Not Hannah or Ruby. No, definitely not them. They share other lives and Jess doesn't want to know. They don't want to know either and haven't done for years.

It is the shark day. May greets her daughters with a frown as they arrive home from the beach. She has heard the shark alarm and demands to know if the girls are all safe.

I hope none of you were in the water when the siren went she says.

No no we weren't Hannah lies. We were all on the beach when it happened mum so don't worry we're fine.

Jess looks down at the scuffed kitchen lino as Hannah blurts this out. She doesn't dare look up in case she gives herself away. But May has other things on her mind now. She is impatient and urgent and frazzled round the edges.

Come along then and have some sandwiches. I've got to get Paul up and bathed before daddy gets home. You know he is finishing early today as he has to go down to his new job soon. We have to finish packing up the house by the end of the week and there is so much to do. Hurry now, there's good girls.

Have you ever noticed how many ugly people there are when you walk down the street? Ugly on the inside. Half of them look like they never smile and that's sad thought Jess.

Take yesterday for example. Bree and Jess had gone to the city to check out the new Docklands precinct. It was a glorious crisp winter day and the sun shone on the water as they walked. Boats of all descriptions bobbed cosily at their berths and the sun sparkled on the new concrete and wooden walkways. Crowds ambled this way and that along the promenade. Jess and Bree thought that with such a glorious setting everyone would be happy. It was Sunday after all and most people were out for a pleasant stroll.

Instead they kept seeing pinched and drawn faces walking past. People who were held tight inside as though they somehow had too much control on things to simply be happy.

I recognised the anguish because I used to be one of them.

Tight and focused and unhappy. Jess knew, believe me she knew.

They wandered from pier to pier and just enjoyed the sunshine and the moment, holding hands and laughing against the breeze.

Look look they cried as each sad face went by. Why are they so miserable on such a day? See the mother over there as she drags her little boy by the hand away from the boats. Away from the water. Away from the sun and the wind and the gulls circling and searching for scraps.

Hurry hurry she calls. Your father is waiting and we have to get back to the car and go home.

But the little boy glances towards Jess and sees her joy and is puzzled for a brief moment. He wants to laugh too but his mother is stern and unforgiving. Come away now we have to go.

Bree and Jess smile at each other and feel a moment of sadness for the little boy who wants to be free but can't. They understand how that feels as they are tugged back to their own childhoods.

Jess is running along the Coogee promenade in the hot summer sun. Ruby and Hannah are nowhere to be seen and for that she is thankful.

I am alone and free!

May had told the girls to be home early from the beach today as there was a lot of last minute packing to be done and she knows that it will be up to her to get things organised. Father will soon be flying down to Melbourne without the rest of the family to start his new job.

I don't understand why we have to move yet again shouts Jess inside her head. She had grown used to this place. Jess liked it here. So did James and Hannah and Ruby. Jess thought her mother liked it here too but you never could tell with her.

She still doesn't laugh much.

But at least May had Paul now and she cherished him. He gets so much attention. More than we ever got, I'm sure thinks Jess to herself. *Especially me who caused my mother such pain.*

But Jess doesn't really worry about the family dynamics as she slows down at the top of the steps. Her bare feet burn for a moment as she dashes across the sand to the water.

Ah, relief! Jess plunges into the sea and is instantly refreshed. She dives and plunges and rolls with the waves. Her strong arms splash confidently as she swims away from the shore.

I am free.

Jess swims for several minutes then halts and treads water. She is beyond the break now and paddling at the back of the crowd. Time stands still, there is nothing but the sea.

Jess feels the sun on her face as she turns on her back to float and drift. Her eyes are closed and she can feel the water in her ears. The sea takes Jess where it will and she is happy. No Hannah or Ruby. No rules. No school bells or demands from teachers. No limits.

Just me and the sea.

Jess feels splashing beside her and opens her eyes. It is one of the surfers paddling out to the big waves. The back set. His board glides past and she watches his feet kick while his arms rise and fall as he paddles. Jess is buoyed by the rhythm of his energy as she begins the slow swim back to the shore.

On the way in Jess tries to body surf a couple of waves. Noone taught her how to do this, she just watched others. Sometimes Jess got hooked on dumpers when it's too late to get off. She could tell by the sand in the curl but usually there's too much momentum to swing out the back of the wave. Dumpers weren't much fun. Jess knew.

Mondays. It's always more difficult to get things flowing smoothly. At least that's what Jess finds these days. Other days you're sort of already into a work routine. But not Mondays. Takes a while to settle.

Jess figured that writing must be one of the greatest passions anyone could have.

Words words words words . . . .

Words. That's what writing is. Telling stories building with them connecting them playing games with them painting pictures with them. At least that's what Jess felt anyway.

Always have. As long as I can remember.

First it was for Jess's survival and nourishment, but she didn't know that as a child.

It was many years later that Jess discovered how important the words were, and she probably had to thank May for that. May and her great big dictionary and her Friday night spelling tests from the primary school grade lists. If it wasn't for May Jess felt sure that she wouldn't have the power of words and the skill to spell them correctly. And maybe that wouldn't matter to most but it sure mattered to Jess.

Arthur loved words too and was a frequent Scrabble player. He liked the written word far more than the spoken word. Jess knew.

Spoken words were usually a signal for some sort of disaster.

Jess tries to delay the inevitable family departure by stalling time. She plays games in her head. She is in denial. Jess builds the words into adventure stories where she is cast as the central character of course. She is brave and intrepid and fearless and totally in command of her destiny.

But it isn't like that at all. Jess is *not* in control. Others are, as usual.

Mother fusses around and as the week progresses and father's departure grows closer she sighs a lot and sucks in her cheeks. She has a look of stoic acceptance pasted onto her face and the children know not to cross her now. They don't argue or question or say too much. It's not worth it.

Jess knows. They all know.

But they also know May is wilting and her strength is beginning to crumble. She is constantly tired and even the baby Paul doesn't keep her entertained any more. There is too much to do and not enough help to do it. May has too much responsibility for the logistics of this major upheaval in her life and why can't Arthur stay a bit longer and set things right? Why is she going to be left alone to finish off as always?

I wish it was Harry with me she thinks bitterly.

Suddenly it is the day of Arthur's departure and the house is in chaos. But Arthur doesn't notice. He's off out of here isn't he? Off to the new job where he'll be met by a driver at the airport.

But the rest of the family will still be here in Coogee thinks Jess.

May pecks Arthur briefly on the cheek as he departs the house. She is forlorn and desperate but Arthur doesn't notice.

The children hang over the front fence and watch him stroll purposefully towards the waiting taxi. Jess feels a sense of abandonment. So much is happening but she cannot take it all in. She wants to see it as an adventure but isn't sure any more if it is. So much is changing.

A part of her feels excitement but also dread. Fear of the unknown. Change. Leaving again.

The sign on the Fruit Shack says brown onions are 39c a kilo but Jess doesn't care. She is sipping her coffee at the carwash café over the road. At the crossroad.

Half my life has come to crossroads of one sort or another.

Choices to be made. Or not.

Sometimes it's easier just to go with the flow and ignore turning left or right Jess muses. She doesn't dwell on whether she's always made the right choices. But she's made them anyway.

Who knows at the time? You just do the best you can.

Jess knew that sometimes there were choices with a capital C that leapt out at you and can't be ignored. Then there are small c choices. Take them or leave them, they don't mind.

But the big C ones can leap out at you at the most unexpected times and bight you in the bum if you ignore them. Jess should know, it'd happened often enough to her.

Like the shark swim. She hadn't see it coming. How could she? Jess was just a kid after all. Sure she knew the risks of the sea and that she was really out too far for someone her age and maybe she should have waited for Hannah or Ruby. But at ten Jess was independent and stubborn to boot. Noone could tell her to stay on shore when the sea was so inviting that day. Besides, Hannah and Ruby were busy with friends and why would they be concerned about their little sister?

When the siren rang that day on Coogee beach so long ago Jess was jolted back to reality damn quick. She knew that somewhere under the water lurked a predator way bigger than her. She realised the danger as she headed madly for the shore but she tried not to panic or to picture the shark. Jess had already heard lots of horror stories like the shark that got into the Coogee swimming pool through the inlet pipe. Shark stories to beach kids are what snake stories are to country kids and Jess was often scared yet enthralled by them. But not enough to stay out of the water for long.

So maybe Jess was lucky that day. Maybe it was only a little c choice to go for that swim but it sure could have had a big C result.

Anyway, back to the onions. Jess gazed across the street to the fruit shack and watched people come and go. A big man wearing a heavy black overcoat goes in. He has a long ponytail. Jess sees him up the street often in the mornings. He takes his elderly mother shopping at Bilo.

Jess is impressed with his dedication and a little bit nostalgic. She wishes it could be her shopping with May, but that part is missing.

Jess never did do much shopping with her mother when May was older. They always lived too far away from each other.

And I guess that was one of those choices too.

But it would have been nice if circumstances had been different Jess reflected.

How could mother and daughter be so far apart in so many ways?

She was my mother after all and that must surely count for something musn't it?

Jess looks in the mirror to search for traces of her mother but there are none that she can recognise. She laughs as she recalls May's attitude to mirrors in her later years. May took all the mirrors down and put them away in boxes. Had none in the house where she'd lived for forty years.

I don't recognise the person I see in the glass, May said. I don't feel like that old white-haired stranger I see. That's not how I feel inside. I'm young still aren't I dear? I only feel sixteen sometimes you know. So young. How could that old face be mine?

Jess studied the reflection of her face and now she can understand what May meant. Age doesn't just glide smoothly along. It creeps up on you and suddenly wham! There you are in the mirror. White-haired and wrinkly.

How in the hell did that happen?

Jess didn't know the answer any more than May but she sure didn't let it get to her. And come to think of it, May could have worried less in her later years about herself and more about her children Jess thought.

Perhaps May tried but it was already too late to rebuild the bridges connecting her offspring. Way, way too late. Even if May *had* crawled out of her inner seclusion in those final years she probably wouldn't have liked what she found.

May was either too alone or too over-burdened or too unaware of other's needs to even try to straddle the middle ground of the fractured family and Jess felt that summed it up.

But there wasn't such a neat package of acceptance in those days when I was the little sister.

Not at all. It was simply damn hard work.

Of course May would always remind her children how hard *she* worked. And how ungrateful they were. And how much she had done as a child for *her* mother and father and brothers.

It is cold when Jess makes her morning entrance in the kitchen so she gathers some kindling and sets the fire. Then Jess flicks on the electric heater and fills the kettle for a morning cuppa. A shiver runs through her as she stoops to set the paper and twigs in the hearth.

The kettle whistles urgently so Jess crosses back to the stove and leaves the fire for now. The heater is already on in the bedroom anyway so Jess heads down the hallway holding tea and coffee in one hand and a jar of dates in the other. Warmth enfolds her as she enters the room and smiles at Bree emerging from under the doona.

Here you are I've made the coffee and I've already set the fire in the kitchen Jess says.

Down the steps to retrieve the morning paper from the dew heavy grass. Thank goodness it is wrapped in plastic! Jess stoops to retrieve the plastic roll then heads back inside.

Back in the warmth of the bedroom she climbs back under the doona and settles in with her tea and the paper. Mack has bounced into the room and is performing his usual morning ritual of eating dates noisily on the bedspread. Jess and Bree both laugh at his antics. They are cosy and happy despite the cold awakening.

What are your plans today Jess asks Bree? Are you over this way at all with work? Maybe you could call in for a cup of coffee later in the morning if you have time?

I'll check my diary Bree replies as she climbs out of bed.

I only have a small diary these days and that's a bonus says Bree. Most days she doesn't even glance at it but it wasn't always that way. Not at all.

Jess used to have a diary too. Large and heavy with a dark blue cover. Full of writing and dates ear-marked and bits of paper jammed in everywhere.

Once upon a time there was a very important person who had lots of commitments and she . . . . gave the impression she was somebody. Know what I mean?

That diary had comments and notes and agendas and meetings and schedules and lots of other information inside. It ran Jess's life and she wanted it run smoothly in those days. Trust her. It did. Jess knew.

Now Jess laughs at the memory of those organised and stressed and routine days and wonders why she thought it was all so important back then. Did she really make a difference at all? Did she achieve what she set out to oh so many years ago when she first entered her profession? *Does it really matter after all she wonders or is it just some useless exercise at massaging the ego?*

Jess's mind comes unstuck a little at the thought that maybe all that energy and all the emotional and personal investment over the years was wasted. But the truth is somewhere in the middle she suspects.

I really don't want to go there. Not today.

Bree is getting ready to leave so Jess sets the match to the fire and puts the toast on. Another cuppa dear she yells out from the kitchen? I've got the fire going so it's nice and warm in here now, there you are.

It is the day the family are leaving Coogee and Jess is sad. Somehow May gets the last of their belongings packed up and sees to the final loading of the household goods then gets everyone into the taxi to the airport. Jess doesn't know how she does it all, what with five children ranging in age from almost one to seventeen.

The children are dressed in their best clothes and shine like ninepins. They have never been on a plane before and are fidgety with nerves and excitement. James knows all about planes and he is busy telling us which are which but noone listens to him. There is too much to do and see and they are all agog.

Here Hannah look after the girls while I take James in to sort out the tickets says mother. Ruby you can hold Paul while I'm gone. All of you sit right there on that grey seat and woe betide you if you move.

May marches off purposefully with James in tow. It is almost comical to see them depart. Nervous May and tall gangly James. Goodness knows how they will sort out our tickets and seats. Jess doesn't understand.

The girls sit and wait patiently with baby Paul. They watch the constant stream of people pass by. It is all a bit daunting.

We are small c city kids after all.

But May somehow manages to get things done and they join a long line of passengers. James looks smug, as though this is all his doing. But the girls know it is not.

Hannah suddenly decides that she wants to go to the toilet and Ruby joins her. Mother is impatient and doesn't want to miss her place in the queue so she installs James firmly in line and marches the three girls towards the nearest rest room. Paul is by now unsettled and cranky and decides to let out a wail of protest at the strange comings and goings of the family. He is too little to understand what is happening but he senses it all the same. He knows something is afoot and he is not happy.

Here Jess you hold him for a bit will you while I make sure we all finish up here as quickly as we can says May urgently.

Jess cradles Paul in her arms, jigging him up and down soothingly. He smells faintly of this morning's milk and cereal as Jess snuggles up to him. He is her favourite and she loves him to bits.

Hannah and Ruby and May all burst from the toilets at the same time and they are ushered back to the queue where James waits. As they near the check in counter mother is nervous and agitated once more. There is too much to do and too much responsibility and she wonders once again why Arthur couldn't be here to help her. It just doesn't seem fair but then life is like that May thinks to herself.

It sure is.

Airports. How much they have changed over the years Jess thinks.

She recalls that first airport experience when the family first flew down to Melbourne so long ago. It would have been Essendon Airport then.

A driver met the family at the airport and drove the family down to Mt Eliza where Arthur worked. Jess thought nothing of it at the time. They stayed six weeks.

The accommodation was like a large hotel and Jess thought it was luxurious. There were lots of rooms to explore and a library and billiard room. Outside were beautiful gardens and lawns and a private beach as well. But the best part was sliding down the grand staircase and going down to dinner in the dining room each night. It was formal with white tablecloths and huge folded napkins. Hannah was beside herself with pleasure. She loved the illusion of grandeur just like Arthur. Must have been the English blood Jess decided.

The grand scale of the place did little for Jess, but it did provide a fresh backdrop to her adventure stories. She was not easily fooled or impressed with the falseties of life like Hannah.

Perhaps I've got more of May's Australia than Arthur's England?

Jess would much rather have been out by herself wandering round the extensive gardens or running down the gravel road to the beach. Alone. Away from *them*.

Ruby and James took it all in their stride and showed their usual lack of enthusiasm and interest of course and Jess didn't expect anything else. That's how they always were, at least around the family anyway. And who could blame them really? After all, as families go ours always was a pretty odd one Jess realised.

Which is why I hid behind the words and used them as my mainstay in life right from my earliest years.

But the new world in which they found themselves down in Mt Eliza wasn't to last for too long after all. It was only a temporary respite from reality while Arthur and May searched for a home.

Six weeks after arriving in Victoria the family moved into a large old weatherboard house in Frankston, where May stayed till the day she died. *In fact she died right there in the loungeroom many years later. But by then she was alone and we had all flown the coop in one way or another. Hadn't we?*

The house had four bedrooms but Jess still had to share. This time it was just Ruby and Jess at first till the others started leaving.

But that was later of course. Much later.

Jess hated sharing with Ruby. She was so messy. She didn't look after anything. Hers or Jess's, it was all the same to Ruby.

Where Jess was neat and tidy Ruby was a slob. Nothing seemed to matter much to Ruby and Jess wondered if it ever would. Ruby seemed to drift along with the wind and it was difficult to pin her down most of the time. *Not that I tried of course. I'd given up by then.*

That's what Jess meant by such an odd family. They were all so *different*. It didn't make sense to Jess and sometimes it still doesn't. But she had long since stopped questioning why and maybe that's a good thing.

It's strange to think that Ruby and Hannah are now the only ones left apart from me. How did that happen wondered Jess?

Arthur decided that seeing he was now earning a good salary it was time to buy the first family car. Jess was eleven years old and it seemed like a dream. She hadn't known anyone in Newcastle or Coogee who owned a car. Jess decided that they must be rich but of course they weren't. Arthur just wanted to impress everyone, May included. That's what Jess decided anyway.

But of course there was a more practical reason for the purchase of the family car. Arthur needed it to get to work. It wasn't about May or the children or trying to pretend. The car was transport, that's all.

Arthur arrived home in the car one night and the family were all amazed. It was a Ford Customline and it seemed huge. It was blue and cream with fins on the back. James was pretty impressed, but Jess knew dad wouldn't let him behind the wheel of this beauty. He would have to wait a while and earn some money of his own before he got wheels.

There were family outings in the car of course. On Sundays there were drives to the Dandenongs with the whole family. At first Jess loved these trips, but later she learned to dread and loathe them. Hannah and Ruby and James usually managed to squirm their way out of them over the years, but Jess was stuck in the back seat for a lot longer.

Probably to look after Paul.

Jess grew to hate the Sunday drives and the babbling river and the tall ferns and the gloomy shade where they would set up the picnic on some rickety old wood table.

It's all so *English* she decided.

Jess would much rather have stayed in Frankston and gone down to the pier for a swim.

The sea is calling me let me go to the sea.

I suppose looking back it's easy to find fault. Arthur was probably just trying in his own way to make things right for the family. Playing the happy father and family man. But for Jess it was too late.

Arthur doted on her spasmodically and tried to make her feel special, but Jess rejected his belated attention.

Even though I had spent years seeking it.

As the youngest daughter Jess had been overlooked for so long that when the attention finally came she found it intrusive and cloying. She didn't feel the need, for the hurt had happened long before. Hadn't it?

Jess no longer went to Frankston. She hadn't for years.

Too many memories and not all of them happy ones.

Not many at all. Happy, that is.

After May died they sold the old house and it became a medical practice. Which is quite ironic when you consider that two of May's brothers were doctors. Go figure.

Bree and Jess called in there one day and stood in the waiting room that was once the lounge. Jess felt weird being back there after so many years away. Over half her life had gone since she'd lived there.

If only these walls could talk. The things this room has seen! You wouldn't believe it.

Jess told them that in fact where they were currently standing was right where May died of a heart attack. Strange that, said Jess. May always said that she wanted to die with her boots on.

Secretly she wanted to die in her beloved garden but it wasn't to be. Aunt Maud was jealous as hell when May fell off the planet so suddenly. She was older after all and she reckoned that she should have gone first. And for May to die so suddenly just like that, well it wasn't right was it?

Be damned if she'd have to do another set of Christmas cards after all Aunt Maud said, but at least she went herself the next year anyway.

Well well we all said at the funeral. At least Aunt M won't have to do the Christmas cards again will she hahah?

It became a family joke of sorts. But there weren't many times the dwindling family got together. Only at funerals.

Hannah got married in this room when I was only thirteen Jess told them. It was a small family wedding at the time. She had to get married they told me but I didn't really understand what they meant.

Hush now they said. It's none of anyone's business but ours.

And who would have thought that all these years later her husband would send Jess such an angry email? You wouldn't read about it would you?

There were other celebrations in the loungeroom of the weatherboard house in Frankston too. A few Christmases. Arthur's work functions. Jess's twenty first birthday. Parties when May and Arthur were overseas. Lots of normal family stuff I guess said Jess.

But there were other things she remembered too.

May died suddenly of a heart attack one wintry afternoon and it was a big shock to the family. Jess got the phone call that night after work. A message from James. Brief and to the point. He'd called in to see May in the weatherboard home in Frankston and there she was. Prone on the loungeroom floor. He'd tried to save her of course and given her the kiss of life while he waited for the ambulance but it was too late anyway. May had gone. When the paramedics finally arrived he slumped beside her body and tried to figure out what to do next. It was taken out of his hands now but at least her demise had been sudden and brief he decided and that was a blessing wasn't it?

Weeks later the adult-children were gathered round May's kitchen table with bits and pieces of their mother's life scattered before them. They had assembled to clean things up and put her affairs in order. James and Hannah and Ruby and Jess.

Paul was dead by then and so was Arthur. The family was shrinking further.

Ruby came down the hall holding Arthur's old leather flying helmet. Look at this she cried, remember this James? Do you want to keep it?

Suddenly James started telling tales about Arthur's flying days. Things Jess'd never heard before. Stories about when he and James used to deliver the newspapers in the Hunter Valley region in a tiger moth. Arthur would load up the papers in the back of the open cockpit and hoist James up on top to act as some sort of ballast.

He would put the helmet on James and pull it down tight over his ears. James reckoned that he did the strap up so tight his eyes nearly bulged out of their sockets. And there he'd be, perched up on top of the papers as they took off with Arthur at the controls as they headed out from Newcastle. James said that he was always mighty pleased when they'd dropped off a few papers as it meant he was sitting lower in the plane. He laughed as he told us the story and Jess wondered if really he'd just made it all up to amuse us. How could these adventures have gone on under my nose as a child without me being aware of them wondered Jess?

See what I mean about an odd family? Bizarre.

They never talked about the things that really mattered and failed to establish a family framework because of the omissions.

Now you understand about the dropped stitches in my life mused Jess. There were whole rows of them let's face it. No wonder Jess was such an erratic knitter.

When Jess was the little sister she developed ways to amuse herself. She had to, noone else would do it for her.

Jess was given a tea set once, she guessed it must have been for Christmas. When it arrived in the grey cardboard box she was so excited. She couldn't wait to open it and admire the shiny colored ceramic pieces that made up the set. They were cream with colored patterns and Jess instantly fell in love with them. It wasn't the cups and saucers and milk jug so much that she admired but what they represented.

They were mine *weren't they?*

Jess spent hours on her own playing with the tea set. She invented a whole host of characters and invited them to elaborate tea parties. She lived in an imaginary world that was so different to the real one, totally immersed in fantasy. She loved every minute of it. Jess could be whoever she wanted to be and create amazing adventures that were all about *her*.

There was no bossy Hannah and no messy Ruby and no teasing James. Just Jess and her adventures.

That tea set was the key to the door of Jess's make-believe world and she looked after it as though her life depended on it.

In Jess's adult mind she can still picture those dainty little pieces as though they are sitting neatly in their grey cardboard box.

I wonder whatever happened to them in the end?

Jess loads more paper into the printer and gazes casually around her office. It was cold this morning so she lit the fire in the kitchen at six a.m. By now the sun will be streaming through the windows on the north side of the house. Jess loves the play of light dancing through the stained glass in the living area. It reminds her of the Newcastle Cathedral windows of her childhood.

Where did that memory suddenly came from?

Strange isn't it how we recall little things at such odd moments in time Jess muses. Take the flying stories that brother James came out with after mother had died. Why did Jess discover those family anecdotes so late in life? Why not when it actually happened?

Perhaps there is a reason for everything but Jess is damned if she knows why. Stories like that would have eased the barrenness of her childhood so why weren't they told?

Her father hadn't encouraged conversation when Jess was young. Arthur preferred hiding behind novels or newsprint. At weekends he'd go out in the garden and push the hand mower round his English lawn. Silly bugger. Wouldn't plant real turf. No, it had to be English. Never really did look any good it was always sparse and spindly Jess thought. But it was his doing and that was what mattered most to Arthur.

After work he'd don his silk smoking jacket and sit in the loungeroom with his sherry and his pipe and the paper. The children dared not interrupt or ask questions about his world. It simply wasn't done. They knew the boundaries and stuck rigidly to them.

Don't upset your father dear you know he's been working hard he needs a rest before dinner now come and help me in the kitchen Jess there's a good girl. She went to help of course. There was no choice was there?

But still Jess wished it could have been otherwise.

Jess is opening the doors in the corridors of her mind. She wonders if she should, not that it really matters to anyone but Jess.

Sometimes it feels like she's back on one of those dumpers at Coogee beach and she sees the sand too late. She can't escape and the inevitable crash is waiting for her.

Another bloody disaster that's what it is.

And you just know that the worst thing of all is that there's always another dumper waiting for you when you least expect it reflects Jess. *Isn't there?*

At least that'd been her experience so far, but over the years Jess'd learned to minimise the damage somewhat. Take the email that was the catalyst, it came completely out of left field.

But it didn't dump Jess in the sand this time, quite the opposite.

It brought Jess some resolution at last.

About bloody time!

But going over family stuff was hard work for Jess. It's patchy and filled with angst, not at all comfortable. Jess tries to dredge up as much as she can to make it all worthwhile.

But sometimes life sure does suck!

Most of her memories are vague yet some are crystal clear.

Maybe I have fabricated most of them after all Jess thinks alarmed. Perhaps Jess has justified the telling now because she'd held things in for long enough and it's time for release. Who knows?

Her father always said to thine own self be true but he wasn't. Not at all. He had two lives Jess discovered.

What are you doing in the bedroom daddy and who is that man you are with?

Jess shivered a little despite the afternoon heat. It was the memory of her childhood that shook her. *That* memory. The one she had tried desperately to suppress.

Daddy daddy I don't understand.

But her eyes had seen his image and there he was before her again all these years after his early death. Jess tried to shut it out even now but she knew it was too strong. Arthur and another man. Together. In bed.

Daddy?

Arthur was a very clever man who was much admired. He had a career life and a family life. He was economist, lecturer, manager, organiser, player, father, husband, brother, son. There were boundaries in his life that he created and the family never crossed.

But Jess was oh so curious in her later years when he was long since gone.

Arthur used to often work till late. *Very* late. May would go to bed and leave her bedside lamp on till he came home.

Jess never did understand why she did that when she knew that it kept her mother awake.

Jess knew that her father would not be home till after midnight so what was he doing all that time? Working late?

Jess didn't think so.

May would never talk about it of course, she was loyal and defensive when ever the subject was raised. Even years after Arthur was dead she would protect his reputation though goodness knows why. Her own mother's stoicism Jess suspected.

Keep a stiff upper lip dear that's what I always say your father was a wonderful man and don't you forget it Jess.

Maybe she was right, but Arthur was only human after all.

And he sure as hell had flaws.

May had once hinted that there'd been others apart from her. If you know what I mean dear she said hardly daring to look at Jess as she spoke. Yes dear there were others and I don't think they were women either she said. If you know what I mean dear.

Men?

Then May would clam up and draw the curtain over her face and her eyes would harden to cold dark pebbles so that Jess knew she would say no more. It was no good trying to get anything much out of May, she simply refused to talk about it. She must have been scared of ruining Tom's name and smudging his reputation.

But you sacrificed your own life too thought Jess.

Jess often wondered over the years who Arthur's men friends were. Perhaps they had been at his funeral? Did they stand in the shadows at the background and shed a silent tear for Arthur the lover?

Jess will never know now. She was only twenty six when he died from a brain tumour.

One day in the summer of his sixty fourth year Arthur came home from work with a headache. He took to his bed immediately which was most unlike him. The silk smoking jacket was left hanging in the cedar wardrobe and his pipe lay idle for the moment.

When May discovered him in bed on her way inside from the garden that day she asked him what he was doing home so early. Aren't you well dear? Did you have a bad day at the office?

I've got a splitting headache he replied. Go away and leave me alone for a while there's a good dear. I'll get up in a bit and have a cup of tea.

But Arthur didn't get up. Not that day or the next. In fact he stayed in bed for most of the next month, refusing to go to the office or do any of the normal things he did.

Jess by then was in Europe travelling with her husband, so she only picked up sketchy accounts of those early days of Arthur's illness later after she'd returned home. At first May sent for the family doctor who diagnosed exhaustion and advised Arthur to stay home and get lots of rest. The headaches were intermittent and he assured May that her husband would be just fine in a little while.

You'll see, the doctor assured May.

But she was a nurse and she wasn't so sure. Something didn't feel right. She just knew it. But of course she soldiered on because that's what her mother had taught her to do hadn't she?

As time passed and with Arthur showing no sign of improvement or of getting out of his bed May began to worry that there might be more to it.

The family doctor suggested that perhaps there was an underlying mental condition behind Arthur's illness, so a psychiatrist was called in to conduct some tests.

Arthur was not himself during this time. His behaviour was strange and inconsistent. His friends and colleagues visited occasionally and a few sent cards wishing him well and a speedy recovery.

Arthur read the cards dutifully then told May to tie them all in black ribbons and send them back. That really got her rattled and she hurriedly sent for the doctor again.

By this time Jess was in the United States and about to embark on a three week Greyhound bus trip when she received a frantic phone call from May. Come home dear come home she sobbed down the telephone. Your father is really bad and I think he'll have to go into hospital and we don't know what's wrong yet and I am very scared.

Jess was pretty rattled by this conversation so she took the next flight home, where she was met at the airport by Hannah and May. It had been a long flight with six stops and Jess was utterly exhausted. Her luggage was missing but at least she was home.

Hullo dear it's so good to have you back and yes we're pleased that you came home and no Arthur's not better at least not yet anyway gushed May. Come on and sit down and let's all have a coffee while we wait to sort out your luggage, Hannah said.

Hannah ushered them over to a nearby table but Jess shrugged her off. She was there for May, not Hannah.

How's dad she asked as they sat down and waited for the coffee? Tell me the latest and where is he now? Which hospital is he in?

Jess had so many questions to ask and so much to catch up on. It had been months since she'd last seen Arthur.

Jess is in grade five at Frankston East primary school and she has made a friend. Her name is Anna and they sit next to each other in an old wooden desk. Jess is getting used to the Victorian school system but finds most of the work too easy. She tries to do her best but it is never good enough for their teacher. Clearly he doesn't like the intruder from another state. He is old and grumpy and Jess doesn't like him either.

One day the class are asked to write a composition. The title is "The Magic Red Boots." Jess is happy for a while as she sets about the task. She loves words and stories and is in her element.

Suddenly the bell rings for lunch time and the teacher tells the class to finish the stories and leave them on his desk. Jess has written such a long and exciting tale. She is still immersed in the words as Anna calls out to her. Come and play with me Jess and we'll sit over here and have our lunch together if you like.

Jess shakes off the story in her head and trots over to where Anna waits by the trees. She is happy. Jess feels accepted, as though she belongs.

After lunch the teacher tells the class that he has corrected their compositions and he will be handing them back after reading. Jess is flushed with excitement as she waits. She knows that her story was well-written and thinks that it must get good marks. It is important to Jess, she wants to be good at something to impress the others in the class.

Mr Wilson strides purposefully up and down the aisles between the rows of desks in the classoom while the students read silently. Noone talks during this time. They all know the rules, and the consequences of breaking them.

The teacher begins to hand out their essays. Jess tries not to look up but she is nervous. He starts with Anna. She gets nine and a half out of ten and Jess is jealous. Mr Wilson thinks Anna is wonderful because she is helpful and neat and clever and smiles at him all the time. Sometimes Jess would like to be more like Anna, but she is not.

Finally Mr Wilson slams Jess's composition down on her desk with a sort of sneer. There! It's done. She is too nervous to look.

Anna turns away as Jess fights back tears. The pages of writing are smudged and covered with angry red lines and marks and swirls. Jess can't believe what she is seeing.

I have only been given four and a half for my beautiful story! How could that be?

Your writing is terrible Jess thunders Mr Wilson. You will have to practice a lot more and why can't you write like Anna?

For a moment Jess is struck dumb there at her desk.

What does he mean my writing is terrible? I wrote the most wonderful story about magic red boots. How could he possibly say it was anything but good?

Then Jess suddenly sees what he had written at the bottom of her work. It was her *handwriting!* It wasn't the story after all that was terrible.

Jess can't believe it still. To have such a wonderful story obliterated by red correction strokes simply because it wasn't in copperplate text? It doesn't make any sense at all to her, but she vows that next time it will be different. He'll see!

And it was. The very next week when the class had composition writing, Jess copied Anna's story word for word. Her beautiful writing and everything. She felt a fraud as she wrote, but Jess was determined to get a good mark.

And I did. Nine out of ten.

There you are Jess I knew you could do it and see how lovely your work is now? Ha ha ha!

Jess smiled as she took the paper from the teacher with somebody else's story written in her hand. She learned an important lesson that day, but it wasn't a positive one. Creativity obviously took a back seat to neatness in that class, and Jess never again wrote such a lovely story whilst in school.

It is cold again this morning and Jess makes some mental plans for the day as she wanders down the hallway to the kitchen. She needs to get things done today, the week is suddenly drawing to an end.

Jess feels a sense of urgency despite knowing at the back of her mind that is silly. There is plenty of time for all her tasks.

Mack comes bounding in as she opens the back door to get some kindling. He leaps and jumps around Jess's feet and she bends down to pat him.

Good dog Mack how are you this morning eh?

Jess wonders what dogs make of this life? She thinks it's strange that people spend so much time with their pets yet never really know what they are thinking? Or *if* they are thinking for that matter.

Jess read somewhere once that back in the stone age the first humans actually learned social behaviour from pack dogs and she wonders if that's true? Maybe it is and maybe it isn't. Jess doesn't know, she wasn't around then. But she figures it makes sense in a way.

Jess glances at Mack and realises how much he means to them. Part of the family now isn't he? They talk to him feed him amuse him play with him take him for walks and love him. Jess knows how lonely they'd be without him now. She remembers other dogs she's owned, there've been a few. Big and small. Country and city. Sacha, Snoopy, Bill, Rex, Gabi, Dude. All wonderful companions and all with their own stories.

And some disasters too.

All gone now except Mack the Wonderdog.

Jess is back in Australia after the trip home from the USA. She finally makes it to the hospital to visit Arthur. Her father.

Daddy dear?

You will notice a change in him dear says May. Be ready.

Jess insists on seeing him alone. She doesn't want Hannah or Ruby or May there for that first visit.

Haven't needed them for years so why would I want them now?

Alright mother Jess says as they climb the wide cold stairs to the ward. Leave me by myself with dad will you? It's been a while since I saw him and I need some time alone with him. I won't be long o.k.?

Jess enters the ward and is immediately struck by how normal Arthur actually looks. She doesn't see much change in him externally anyway. *He looks almost the same to me.*

Hi there dad how are you and what are you doing in here? How are they treating you then alright?

Jess leans over and gives Arthur a brief hug. He smells faintly of his old self but hospital smells have overtaken him a little in his starched white bed. He is slightly dishevelled but Jess overlooks this for now. He would hate that though, Arthur has always been fastidious about his appearance. No silk smoking jackets and evening pipe and sherry in here of course. He is just another patient now and he would hate that too. Always wanted to be *someone*.

Hullo darling he says as he turns towards Jess. How was your trip and where is that husband of yours? Did he come home with you?

Jess tells Arthur that her husband stayed on overseas for a bit but he doesn't acknowledge her. Arthur hasn't got his hearing aide in and perhaps he doesn't hear. Where is he then he asks?

Jess clasps her father's hand briefly and it feels cold. The veins stand out and she suddenly notices how frail he seems.

Arthur looks suddenly old and helpless and Jess tries to rationalise this man in the bed with the person she knows is her father.

How could that be, what has happened here?

Later the same thing would happen to Maud his sister when she went in to hospital for the last time. But that was much much later, wasn't it?

Can I get you anything dad are you comfortable Jess asks quietly?

Nonono. Leave me be dear. They'll let me go home soon you know I'm sure of it.

I don't think so.

But Jess doesn't say this to Arthur, she tries to humour him along with a few anecdotes from her recent travels. Arthur is well-read and articulate and he likes a good story. He's travelled a bit too so father and daughter have something else in common now. Jess gets a laugh from him at some of her travel anecdotes and she sees the old Arthur emerge from the shadows once more. She feels comforted a little now that he seems his old self again.

But it doesn't last long of course.

Soon the family hears the diagnosis that they had all been dreading. Inoperable tumour. Terminal. A matter of weeks or a month or two at the most. Sorry. Sorry sorry sorry.

I'll bet Arthur is sorry too but he doesn't really show it. Jess is sure he knows that he is dying, probably has all along.

Just tie black ribbons round the cards and send them back.

Sometimes the journey is about everything and sometimes it is about nothing. Steps along the way. Jess tells her friends that she is writing a novel and they look at her askance and say good for you Jess what is it about?

If she tells them it's an autobiography they gaze at her and say my my aren't you brave? So she tells them it's a story about one woman's journey of self-discovery and they tut tut and titter at her as though she speaks another language.

So I don't tell them anything. I change the subject.

Jess and Bree are at another retirement dinner. A former colleague.

Ho hum.

When they arrive Jess is immediately struck by the distance she has created between her past and present lives.

How and why did I ever exist in the falseness of this world?

Jess glances around the crowded room taking it all in. A sea of mouths and faces and bobbing heads. Glasses of chardonnay and champagne rise and fall amid the din of laughter and conversation and tight grins and titters and guffaws. Glances are thrown here and there as the triers and the wannabes and the has-beens all seek each other's attention.

Look at me look at me! I am someone *aren't I?*

All the women have dyed hair and the obligatory black outfits and false smiles and flashing white teeth that bray like fretful fillies there in the holding pens. There are clones of themselves everywhere if only they could see. But they don't of course. They are far too busy socialising and being important. They drape themselves across each other's shoulders like grandma's old shawl and dribble and pout at each other while secretly despising every other female in the room.

They are networking darling and don't you just feel the love? They are just so full of crap.

The men are no better of course but they attack the evening in a different way. All beer and balls and bravado. D'jer hear the one about Jonesie eh, what a ripper?

Nudge nudge wink wink.

The upwardly mobiles hide beneath suits and ties and crisp colored collars but their intent is just the same as the women. A word in the right ear here and there and a reference to a job well done. Drop a name or two in the right place. Mention that conference last week and wasn't the keynote speaker so right about the latest trends mate? Have another beer or would you rather a red? I'll get them mate she's right!

The already-retired ones of course are there as well, bathing in the warm fug of yesterdays. Suits abandoned for casual jumpers and trousers and open necked shirts. Caught midway between where they once were and where they are now. Stuck nowhere. Not really where they want to be at all. Played any golf lately they ask each other aimlessly? What's your handicap these days eh?

Bloody life. That's *their handicap.*

But they can't quite work out why they feel a pinch or two of discontent and envy as they wander round the room seeking something that they've lost. Shelter from the storm. Solace. *Belonging.*

But they *don't* belong any more and they know it. Part of them wants to and another part says stuff it. We've been there and paid our dues haven't we? But why in the hell do they feel so useless?

Stuff it, let's have another beer. G'day Bazza mate remember me?

Jess joins a group of former colleagues who are now friends. They are catching up on old times.

Family travel fun times. An arm comes over her shoulder and a harsh voice shrieks in Jess's ear, cutting across the conversation.

Hullo Jess is that you how are you?

Huh?

Jess turns around and catches a glimpse of her former employer.

There is nothing I want to say to you, go away go away!

Jess turns away and resumes the conversation.

I'm out of the loop darling I want to yell at her. Can't you see I'm no longer part of this crappy networking scene? Go away go away.

They are serving finger food and Jess suddenly realises how hungry she is after the long drive to town.

Maybe the energy has been sucked out of me by all this shallowness. Anyone for canapés darlings?

For Jess's twelfth birthday Arthur decides to give her a bicycle. Not a new one of course, but Jess doesn't mind. It's has been re-conditioned and painted bright green.

Irish green May would say. Kelly green says Arthur.

But Jess doesn't mind what green it is. It's a pair of wheels, her ticket to freedom and adventure.

Jess is now in grade six and it is mid year. School has become boring.

She is more interested in other pursuits and is impatient and restless and full of energy. Jess hates walking to school each day but at least she still has Anna as a friend. They sit together and share stories and playground fun.

Jess has developed a love of horses. Over the back of their house is a dairy which still uses horses to deliver the morning milk. Jess spends hours sitting on the back fence watching the horses snort and roll and trot around their small paddock. There are about twenty of them and she gives each of them a name. They are black and brown and piebald and skewbald. They become her friends too, a part of Jess's world.

As time goes by Jess become more adventurous and begins to hang around the stables and help the stablehands. She sits on the horses in their stalls and helps brush them and put their gear away.

The horses steam and smell when they come back to the stables after their morning work, but Jess soaks it all in. She immerses herself in the horse world as though she somehow belongs.

One morning Jess is at the stables cleaning some harness and singing away happily to herself. She is in the tack room and can smell the horses as they stomp and snort in their stalls. It is warm and fetid but Jess doesn't mind. She loves it here.

As Jess reaches up to get a bridle off one of the hooks she suddenly senses danger. Jess is gripped in a vice-like hold and smells stale sweat. She's not sure what is happening but it feels bad.

The old stablehand has snuck up and grabbed her from behind and she feels his strong arms and smells his hot horrible man smell. He pulls Jess's young body close to his and she is sick with fear and dread and the fright of the unknown. Jess tries to cry out but her throat has gone dry and all that emerges is muffled silence.

Suddenly something snaps in Jess and she fights free from his grip. She turns and runs from the stables, choking with revulsion as she flees. Away away without slowing or looking back. The tears run fast down her face as she finally stops to hide herself in the safety of a large old tree.

Bastard bloody bastard Jess yells out loud to noone at all. Shit bugger bum!

Jess brushes herself down and lies there in the cool grass for what seems like forever. Time passes by. Jess doesn't want to go home. She doesn't want to go anywhere. Something has shifted in her world and Jess doesn't know what it is.

But I know I don't like it at all.

The smell of baking bread greets Jess and Bree as they return from the city. It is late and they are tired from the long drive. Bree calls out from the bedroom as Jess puts on a pot of fresh coffee.

Would you like some bread and vegemite with your coffee dear?

Sounds good Bree replies, it smells great.

They sit by the electric heater with their toes on the old brick hearth.

The wood fire has gone out but they sit there anyway.

What a night Jess says to Bree. Did you enjoy yourself? What a hoot!

All those people pretending to be important! Funny wasn't it? If only they could see themselves!

They laugh at each other and talk about the night in the city. It's rather odd that I used to be a part of it too don't you think Jess says to Bree. *God how did I do that for all those years? Go figure.*

They chat for a while as they munch on the hot bread and slurp the hot coffee, then decide it's time for bed. God we're just like a couple of old farts says Jess and they crack up laughing.

Oh well, who cares anyway says Bree, I'd rather be an old fart with our lifestyle now than any of those people who were there tonight wouldn't you?

Got that in one, snorts Jess. No way am I doing the networking career look at me I'm so important thing again, that's for sure. Hell will freeze over first!

They both giggle as Jess turns out the light.

Night night dear.

Some people can freeze-dry their entire lives into neat tidy packages, but I'm not one of them thinks Jess.

I'm still knitting.

Let's face it nothing ever goes to plan if you really think about it and that's the trouble with thinking. Does your head in at times. Jess knew.

But where would we be without the odd pause here and there along life's highway to stop and wonder about things Jess asks herself?

To look around and simply ask *why?*

Maybe there have been too many whys in Jess's life but she can't change that now.

Fact. I can't erase the past even if I wanted to so what the hell?

But don't you ever wish that you could do things over, Jess shouts?

Jess feels sure that May would have done things differently second time around, but she was never brave enough to try.

What would she have done differently if she'd started over?

Harry. Maybe May would have chosen Harry instead of Arthur.

Children. Maybe she'd have had fewer given the opportunity.

Career. Perhaps she'd have continued with her nursing.

Her mother. Maybe, just maybe, May might have defied her after all and not been the dutiful daughter all those years. Such a waste!

Jess is pulling at fragments and dropping too many stitches. She feels the tension of anxiety approaching.

I don't need that now, not today.

The clock of Jess's life is ticking away loudly and she's not too sure where it is leading her. She needs to resume control and get on with things. Jess is a doer not a dreamer.

Once all she had were dreams to sustain her. Fantasy and imagination. Words. Words words words.

Down by the station early in the morning.

Jess had songs and chants and poetry in her head right from the start.

See the little puffing billies all in a row.

Thank you thank you word god!

Jess is dropping too many stitches in the telling. Her mind is jumpy and she needs to concentrate.

Focus dear, that's what mother would say. Stop wasting time and get on with it Jess!

But May wasn't always right, Jess knows she wasn't.

Her life was mostly a ruin of other people's dreams so what right did she have to dictate to me?

As far as Jess could recall May was at everyone's beck and call for most of her life until she grew old. Until she found some peace and freedom. Finally finally it happened.

But who knows if she ever found true happiness?

May never confided in Jess and she never really expected her to. But a part of Jess wished it could have been different. A sharing of sorts.

Even a gesture would have appeased Jess before May died. A symbol or a token of the mother-daughter bond.

Something.

But what little May did give wasn't enough and Jess can't change that now.

Too late too late isn't it?

Perhaps I am being over sensitive and unforgiving muses Jess.

May tried in her own way to reach out at times to Jess, but it wasn't enough to make up for the past and that was the problem.

And of course it wasn't May's problem but Jess's in the end. There were simply too many dropped stitches along the way that Jess couldn't pick up.

Too many arguments and slammed doors and pleading phonecalls and abrupt dismissals and rejections and lack of interest and tears and shouts and anger and coldness. Wasn't there?

You know I love you dear and by the way are you coming home for Christmas asked May? No I can't possibly come up and help you with the new baby dear I've got the electrician coming this week.

Other mothers helped their daughters and maybe Jess's did too but why didn't Jess *feel* anything in the end?

With May it was all about duty not love, at least that's how it seemed to Jess and that's all she had to go on wasn't it?

Maybe it was different for the others. For Hannah and James and Ruby and Paul.

But they weren't Jess.

Jess is almost at the end of grade six and beginning to spread her wings a little. Anna is in the marching girls and Jess asks May if she can join too. But May says no, they are nothing but brazen hussies.

Jess doesn't know how May knows this, she doesn't even know what a brazen hussy is. But she knows May will not change her mind, she rarely does.

Then one day when Jess is out riding her bike she passes an oval where kids are riding round doing tricks. She stops to watch, fascinated.

Jess discovers that it is the Pedal Club and she instantly wants to join. She could finally be part of something. Something that doesn't involve Hannah or Ruby or James. Or even baby Paul for that matter, though he is still her favourite.

That night after dinner Jess does the dishes promptly without being reminded and fetches Arthur his pipe. She sits quietly in the loungeroom and waits for the opportunity to raise the subject of the Pedal Club.

Finally Jess speaks into the silence of Arthur's smoke.

Dad can I talk to you for a minute Jess blurts out. I saw these kids today riding bikes and I want to join this club they have. It's on an oval and it's safe and it's called the Pedal Club. There are adults there supervising and it looks like lots of fun. Can I can I please?

To Jess's surprise Arthur glances at her over the rim of his glasses and looks at May.

They smile at each other indulgently and say what do you think dear will we let her join? It sounds harmless enough.

Alright Jess we'll come down and see what it's like next Saturday dear, now off you go and do your homework there's a good girl. Where's the paper dear I want to have a look at the business page and check my shares dear oh there it is mumbles Arthur.

Jess can't believe it! They have given her permission to join something finally. She is rapturous with joy as she retreats to her bedroom, but she doesn't say anything to her sisters. Jess knows this will bring scorn and teasing from them so she avoids their glances and keeps the happiness inside. Jess has played the game again on her terms and this time she has won!

I can't wait to see Anna at school tomorrow and tell her the good news.

Ruby is in the bedroom lying on Jess's bed and has messed it all up.

Of course. She doesn't care.

Sometimes Jess thinks that Ruby does it to spite her and sometimes it's just because she has no boundaries. Nothing seems to phase Ruby so it doesn't matter to her who's bed she's on. But it matters to Jess and Ruby knows that.

For now Jess tries not to let it spoil the joy of the moment but a small part of her is angry nonetheless.

I can't help it. I am not like Ruby and I hate untidiness.

Jess realises that she has probably inherited the tidy gene from Arthur and not from May, but it doesn't really matter except to her.

It is a public holiday and Bree and Jess luxuriate in the warmth of their bed with the paper and their toast and coffee. Mack lies at their feet as they read and listen to the news. It is cold outside and they don't want to face the outdoors yet. Their little heater with the imitation fire provides comfort and warmth.

What do you feel like doing today dear Jess asks? Shall we go for a drive down to Portarlington and catch some of the music festival later? We could have a coffee down there at that yummy bakery. What do you think Bree? The sun might come out later on.

Yes yes she says. Let's do that then. I'll get up soon and make a fresh pot of coffee if you like smiles Bree.

Okay then I'll light the fire in the kitchen and we can sit out there and finish breakfast, alright asks Jess?

Jess chuckles to herself as she wanders down the hallway to the den. We *are* just like a couple of old farts she thinks.

Hahaha. To think I'd ever be like this well I never dear! Whatever has happened to me?

Where has the time gone do you suppose Jess muses? Gawd I sound just like May and *that's* pretty scary.

Let's not go there nonono.

Would you like another piece of toast Jess calls out to Bree as she sets the fire. I've got the kindling in dear and the fire is ready.

But somewhere in the back of her skull Jess feels that old déjà vu thing happening.

I know I've done this all before. Haven't I?

Bloody technology. Who says it makes life easier? In some respects maybe but it can also be a complete pain in the butt. Jess knew from bitter experience.

Jess had been talking to a friend on the phone last Sunday morning and the conversation veered into the technology stuff. I got my Optus phone bill the other day Jess tells her.

I've joined a new $99 plan so I get a bill for $177. How does that work Jess asks? And to cap it off says Jess, the damn phone calls only amount to a total of $14! What's the rest for? Convenience?

I smell a rat her friend snorts down the line indignantly.

I smell a whole room full of rats Jess replies.

The Optus gods must be pretty pleased with themselves she says. They're making bucket loads of money and it's all going to Singapore, don't you just love it?

The Telstra phone beside my bed has stopped working Jess adds. At least it allows me to receive calls but not make them.

Jess laughs down the phone and says that the Telstra god must have stopped talking to the Optus god.

I'm sure that's right her friend yells back. And the damn Dodo god has stopped working all together and won't give me my usual path to the universe on the internet.

The two friends laugh at the technology gods till they are fit to burst.

I think you should get a couple of tin cans and some string Jess, or maybe a pigeon, that'll do the trick. Bugger technology!

What a good idea Jess responds. We've got a few pigeons out the back, they eat Mack's tea every night. And if the bloody things don't do their job I can turn the tables and feed *them* to the dog hahaha.

Anyway it's just as well we can see the funny side eh laughs Jess?

Then the friend suddenly says have you got the twenty minute plan Jess because we've been on the phone for a while? Hang up and I'll call you back, that's what you do she says. You can talk for ages as long as it's in twenty minute lots.

The twenty minute plan Jess asks? Hell I'm on the Optus One plan for $99 that costs me $177 so don't ask me what the hell I know about plans screams Jess. All I know is that if you dare to change the damn plan to get something cheaper they charge you an arm and a leg and it ends up costing you more. True, Jess tells her. Just ask the Optus god, they'll tell you. Hahaha.

When I phone my son it's only on the mobile Jess tells her friend. That's the way it is these days, noone uses landlines any more for some strange reason. It's all sms texting or voicemail or email. Whatever. Beeps on the mobile at all hours to tell you that someone has sent you a message but noone has talked to you wails Jess.

Don't be silly we don't use voices any more.

I phoned number one son recently at home on his landline Jess tells her friend, and he picked it up and said gruffly down the line why are you calling the home number?

Because you are home Jess said lamely, thinking that there was logic in her response.

But I might have been out he says, use the mobile for god's sake mum. Then I would have left a message on messagebank Jess had replied.

But she knew it was a lost cause by then, he thinks she's a goner when it comes to the joys of modern technology despite the fact that Jess has mastered sms and email.

Oh well, there's no accounting for it is there?

Take last night for example guffaws Jess. My son phones me at home, a rare enough event, and says Hi I didn't get your voicemail till Sunday.

That's o.k. Jess says and did you get the sms I sent on Saturday night about the footy?

I ignored that replies number one son indignantly. You're hopeless any way mum when it comes to footy!

Thanks for nothing Jess replies. Hahaha.

Anyway, I am talking to him last night on the mobile in my kitchen Jess screeches down the phone. I can't hear you I say the phone is all crackly.

It must be your end he says. I can hear you just fine.

Oh no, Jess thinks, now the Nokia god is giving me a hard time.

Hang on Jess yells, I'll hang up and call you back on the other phone. I'll just grab the cordless!

Alright he says with a degree of pity, if you must.

See what I mean about making things harder says Jess to her friend? Too many plans and systems and pieces of plastic technology floating round in the universe and not communicating with each other.

Bloody technology gods. I hate them!

I have to go now mum he says down the line as Jess finally manages to get a good signal without crackling or inteference. I've got to get out to the airport to pick up my wife.

I'll call you on Saturday Jess replies as the phone goes dead in her hand. *Bye!*

May decides that Jess should learn the piano. They have a large black piano in the loungeroom. Beckman. New York.

Sometimes when May is playing Jess hears happy tunes emerging from the room. But often they are sad and whistful.

In the mornings May just plays scales. Up and down. Down and up. Fast medium slow.

Jess has long been fascinated by May's ability to play the piano, so her parents take this as a signal that she wants to learn to play. Which Jess does in a way but she doesn't realise how much practice this entails. *Hours and hours and hours.*

Are you sure you want to learn Jess, May asks? You know it will cost us quite a bit of money so you will have to practice every day dear she says.

Yes yes mum I will responds Jess eagerly, thinking to herself that in a short time she will be able to play tunes and songs like May.

It'll be fun, Jess thinks, and it's something that none of the others can do so I will have one up on them.

Haha Hannah and Ruby and James. Hahaha.

Any small victory over the sisters and brothers is huge for Jess.

I won't be the little sister will I? I will do something they can't.

And it turns out to be true. Jess *did* have a natural aptitude for the piano and she managed to complete up to grade five in only three years. But by then other aspects of her life had taken over and she was no longer interested in the hours of daily practice.

Jess wanted more freedom, she didn't want to continue the weekly bike ride at 6.30a.m. to the piano lessons. Especially in winter when it was cold and dark. And she most certainly did *not* want a repeat performance of wearing a white dress and going to the city to play in an eisteddfod, even if it was on a grand piano.

But of course Arthur and May were none too pleased with Jess's decision to quit piano. Nor was the elderly tutor who'd trained in London all those years ago and recognised her talent.

What a waste he said as he pleaded with May to keep Jess there. She is a natural he said. She should keep going.

No mother, Jess said as she stamped her feet. It's a waste of good money and I'd much rather be out doing other things.

Why can't I have a horse instead?

Well I never replied mother, did you hear that Arthur? What an ungrateful child you are Jess and after all we've done for you. A horse? Really!

Jess knew it would never happen of course even if she had kept going to piano lessons. Even if she had kept practicing and learning music theory. There was no way they would ever agree to a horse despite Jess's fervent wishes. It was simply out of the question. She would have to ride horses where she could.

But they always belonged to others and not to Jess.

Sometimes we fall in love for the right reasons and sometimes not reflected Jess one dull Autumn afternoon.

Nobody wrote the rules as far as I know so who knows why?

May always said live and learn but Jess wasn't sure that May had over all those years. Maybe she did learn from life experiences but May sure had a lot of bitterness to show for it didn't she?

Love is a lot like life Jess believes. Lots of dropped stitches and added rows here and there and tangled skeins of colored wool draped around your feet. At least that's how Jess'd found it but she supposed other people had different views.

May always said she'd loved Harry yet she fell in love with Arthur too. And in his own possessive way Jess knew that Arthur had desperately loved May way back at the beginning. He used to write her romantic poetry. Jess knew because she still had most of them stored away in a battered old manila folder in the office shelves. A testament to raw emotion and desperation. Arthur's desire.

Or folly decided Jess.

May remained loyal and true to Arthur over the long years of their marriage for reasons that only she could understand. Jess guessed a lot of it came down to expectations in those days. May's mother's and Arthur's, and even her own.

But Jess suspected that if she'd had her time again May might have done things much differently and maybe felt more joy along the way.

Who knows?

Sometimes at the oddest moments Jess would catch a glint of something resembling love pass between her parents but perhaps she was mistaken after all. Jess didn't understand such things when she was young.

Jess's baby brother Paul died alone in the early hours of a December morning.

He wasn't a baby by then though was he? Twenty one he was.

It was two days before Christmas. Paul was riding his motorbike and hit the steel barrier of a T intersection at one in the morning. He'd been drinking at a party and he should never have got on his bike. He rode away fast. Very fast. He hadn't even applied the brakes.

What does that tell you Jess?

It was two a.m. when there was a persistent knock at May's front door. Jess was staying there with her husband and two children at the time. They were down for Christmas to catch up with the family.

What's that Jess mumbled as she stirred suddenly from sleep? Who's there?

Jess stumbled to the front door, opening it slightly but leaving the chain on. A young policeman was standing there caught in the front porchlight. He looked so serious and forlorn, as though he'd rather be anywhere else right at this given moment.

Are you related to Paul he asked?

What what what?

Jess was frozen still there at the door. Has something happened to him?

Is he dead?

The policeman looked awkward as he answered in the affirmative.

How could that be? Nonononono!

Jess invited the young policeman in and they stood in the hallway as he briefly outlined the details of Paul's recent and sudden death. Her husband joined Jess as they spoke about the recent tragedy. Jess's life seemed on hold. It was too surreal. She was in shock.

All Jess could hear were staccato words that seemed to be coming from somewhere a long way away. Echoes down a long corridor.

It wasn't happening to us, was it?

Speed, motorbike, alcohol, party, friends, loud revving, screeches, crashing noises, darkness, body, morgue, identification. *What?*

Jess remembers feeling numbness and incredible loss at the time. How could her favourite baby brother be dead? How could he disappear from their lives just like that? In an instant. It didn't seem real, how could it be? Jess'd seen him only that afternoon when he'd come round to say hi and use mum's clothes dryer. Hadn't he?

Then she remembered the argument he'd had with May. So stupid and so trivial, she'd abused him for using the clothes dryer! May told her youngest son that he'd left home now and what right did he have to use her things? Who would believe it? How could May be so petty? She was his *mother* for god's sake!

Paul had stormed out with anger hanging in the air and harsh words following him out the door.

Would that be Paul's lasting legacy for his mother?

May had gone back outside to the garden with a cup of tea and ignored the damage she'd caused, hadn't she?

And now she'd never see her youngest son alive again. He was gone. *Taken from all of us wasn't he?*

How utterly senseless Jess thought to herself.

If only she'd left him alone. He had still been so young!

It was a terrible Christmas that year.

See what I mean about disasters?

Jess knew there were times when things go wrong and they are simply beyond your control. Take yesterday for example. There she was tapping away happily at the computer when suddenly the damn thing froze. Kaput. Just like that.

See what I mean about technology?

This time it was the Toshiba god that was giving Jess a hard time.

Bloody bugger bum she yelled out to noone in particular as she sat and stared at the screen helplessly. Which of these buttons do I press to bring the laptop back to life? Ctrl Alt del. That should do it.

Click, hold, release.

Whirrr! The green light flickers on and off. But nothing happens. The damn thing's still frozen.

Try F2 or F3 Jess reasons, maybe that'll work. Tap tap hold. Flickering green light again but no luck. Still Jess can't find the cursor or the arrow. Gone. Disappeared into the universe somewhere up there with the other technology gods. Perhaps they are having an in-service somewhere out there in space.

Maybe the Toshiba god is conferring with the Dodo god and the Optus god and the Telstra god. They are all up there somewhere laughing at me thinks Jess. Hahaha. I guess there is an element of humour there but it doesn't help to retrieve the words, does it?

Jess leaves the laptop on and drives down to the computer shop.

Maybe they can help me?

Hi, Jess says, remember me? You did an upgrade for me a couple of months back. I'm having some problems with the Toshiba and it froze. What can I do to fix it?

Jess looks imploringly at the sales assistant who seems to be about primary school age. But he is tolerant and helpful and very savvy when it comes to dealing with older customers like Jess.

Let's face it, there must be enough of us. Oldies I mean. Baby boomers.

Well have you tried pressing ctrl-alt-delete? That didn't work? Hmm. Try it again and if it still doesn't work I'm afraid you'll have to just shut it down and re-boot it again after a bit he says. You'll lose anything that wasn't saved he adds.

Damn! Jess doesn't want to hear that. Two pages of work down the drain. *Bugger! Bloody technology I say.*

The young assistant smiles at Jess condescendingly, as though he is used to the vagaries and inefficiencies of the older generation who grew up without computers. Or mobiles or ipods or mp3 players or dvd's.

Jess was already twelve when tv first came to Australia for god's sake. *Try telling him that though.*

Bree and Jess go for a stroll down to the river with Mack. Past the shops and K mart and through the park. They let Mack off the lead and he runs and runs. He chases birds but he never catches them. They always fly off and Mack can never work out where they go. Funny dog.

Look at him go Jess says to Bree and they both laugh at his antics.

He's better than a circus that dog, fair dinkum he is.

Here boy come here Jess calls out as they near the road.

Mack's small black and white figure emerges from behind a large gum tree.

Here boy come and get your lead on, calls Jess.

They stop at the traffic lights and press the pedestrian button.

Click click click.

Cars swing round the bend in front of them as they wait. Mack pulls at the lead impatiently but Jess tightens her grip and tells him to stay. He looks at her as though he understands but Jess doesn't really think so.

Not Mack.

Here we go Bree says as the lights change. Let's go.

They cross the river on the narrow footpath with cars whizzing close by. Mack doesn't like the bridge. He can see the river below and feels anxious. He hates bridges and piers and walking above water.

Come on boy, Jess calls. It's alright. We're nearly over the other side.

They reach the car yard and notice a new model Holden. That's a smart looking car Bree says, I saw one of those driving round the other day when I was in the city. Pretty zappy don't you think?

Let's go across the road and have a coffee Jess replies. We can tie Mack up and have a wander round the garden section while we're there. Okay?

Jess couldn't believe Paul had gone. Surely that wasn't so?

They were back home in the country, Jess and her husband and two small children.

Jess had picked up the fallen stitches and was knitting the jumper of her life once more but it seemed harder somehow. The rows weren't even and the stitches seemed all different sizes, as though she didn't have control of them any more. Jess's life felt empty and out of control. Her marriage felt the same.

Jess tried hard of course to make things work.

But sometimes trying isn't enough is it?

Jess knew that there were times when parts of your life just slid further and further downhill despite good intentions.

That's what I mean about disaster, it sneaks up on you and lies in wait no matter what you do.

What Jess did was drink. That'll help to make me feel good, she thought. That'll lift my spirits and take me into happy land won't it reasoned Jess? Have another wine Jess there you go dear isn't that great and don't you just feel the love? Nothing like a glass or two of cask wine is there dear hahaha? Gedidinderya!

And of course at first it *was* only a glass or two and that was fine.

Jess would take a sip from the cask while preparing the evening meal. Nothing wrong with that is there girl?

How's your day been dear and what did you do today?

How are the kids her husband would ask as he came in the door after work? Were they good today dear and by the way would you like another wine hoho?

So when did the drinking problem really begin? When did Jess realise that it was taking over her life? How many casks and years later did Jess accept that she had a drinking problem despite what everyone else said?

Don't be silly Jess you don't drink that much and anyway we all drink don't we dear? Come on have anothery.

Yes yes Jess responded, but we don't all have the bad nights that I do and the days filled with remorse and the embarrassment of being drunk in front of the children and thinking after all it's such a little thing. Isn't it? *Look at me children aren't I funny don't you think mummy is such a clown hahaha?*

One night when Jess was alone and her husband had finally left she dropped all the stitches. Jess was drunk and maudlin and suffering from acute anxiety. At 3a.m. she found herself curled up in a foetal position on the kitchen floor sobbing. Something in Jess snapped and she howled, *Enough!*

Jess decided then and there that she would have to somehow fix this problem, she couldn't go on like this. She had to clean up her act and get help to stop drinking before it totally ruined her life.

Whatever it took, Jess decided she would work to regain control of her life.

She deserved that much and so did her kids.

One night Jess woke in the middle of a strange dream. It was her bladder that stirred her from sleep of course, but the dream was still draped around her as she padded down the hall to the toilet. Through the den and the kitchen and the laundry.

Why are you smiling at me daddy dear and who is that man in the background?

Back in bed once more Jess pulled the covers over her head so that only a small part of her face was exposed to the cold night air. It reminded Jess of those freezing winter nights in the valley years ago.

I'm so glad we now live by the sea. Lucky lucky.

But the dream was still there and Jess couldn't shake it off. There was a paddock of dried grass and the sun shone down to create one of those heat hazes you get on hot summer days in the country. Jess was there to meet strangers who were dressed in cowboy outfits. They were on horseback riding towards her.

They told Jess that there was going to be a big business merger or takeover happening and she had to sign the papers or the whole deal would fall through.

Go figure, I don't even own shares.

Sometimes you can examine your dreams and kind of work out what they mean Jess thought. Or what you *think* they might mean anyhow. But this one didn't make any sense, so she let it slide away into oblivion.

Maybe the dream gods are a bit like the technology gods. Maybe not. I'm sure they aren't there to make a profit after all.

The day after Jess's drinking session she took the plunge and walked into the local doctor's office.

I think I'm drinking too much and I want to do something about it. I feel like it's out of control and I need to stop, Jess blurted out.

Before she knew what was happening the doctor was speaking to someone on the phone.

It's alcoholics anonymous for god's sake and Jess is panicking and screaming in her head *Nonono I don't need them!*

But she sits there subdued and stares at a picture on the wall while the doctor finishes the call. Then he looks across at Jess and says that there is a meeting this week that he wants her to go to. She will be picked up and taken there by someone. It is all arranged, okay Jess?

Okay? You've got to be kidding me!

In her head Jess is a mess. She convinces herself that the doctor must have made a mistake.

I'm not an alcoholic, I just drink a little bit too often. Don't I?

Well well he says to me. How do you feel about that Jess?

Well I don't know how I feel Jess tells him.

But inside I'm scared. Damn scared. Another disaster with a capital D.

It's like, uh oh, here we go again Jess!

Jess smiles weakly at the doctor and tells him that it will be alright, she'll go to the AA meeting just to see what it's all about if that's what he thinks she should do.

Maybe it's what I need after all?

Sometimes life can be like sitting in the outfield waiting for the fly ball to land. Holding your glove out and hoping like crazy you can catch it and not drop it. Waiting and hoping. Watching intently full of unexplained expectations. Wishing you were somewhere else maybe and worrying that you're not. Caught midway.

It was like that for Jess when she went to that damn AA meeting all those years ago. She was nervous as hell but she didn't let on of course. Jess really believed in her heart that she shouldn't be there. After all, she wasn't an alcoholic.

Was I?

But she went anyway because she'd given her word and Jess almost never backed out of things. She stuck with the commitment despite severe misgivings, but it sure felt weird going to that meeting.

Here we are then says Bert. We're here.

Well I can see that replies Jess with disdain, trying to act nonchalant. But in her head Jess wants to yell at him and tell him there's been a mistake. He's got the wrong person.

Take me home Jess wanted to cry out, I don't want to go to this crummy meeting after all.

But it's too late for that so Jess follows Bert inside. They pass through to a small meeting room where about a dozen people are sitting on chairs in a circle. Jess tries to avoid their gaze, she feels like an imposter to be honest. An outsider.

Nonono! Why are you all staring at me?

But they are not staring at Jess of course. They are warm and friendly and welcoming, trying to invite her into their circle.

I don't want to be part of this, I want to go home! Help!

The ritual begins but Jess is choking back tears of frustration and she cannot hear the words. She sees the mouths around her moving but she is struck dumb with the fear of the unknown and cannot respond.

Once upon a time . . . . aaagh!

Arthur had come home early from the office and found the house empty. As he idled into the carport and cut the motor he remembered that May and the children had gone to the city for the day. The place seemed oddly quiet for a weekday but secretly Arthur was pleased. More than that, he was delighted.

Home alone for once, how pleasant.

Just as he entered through the front door the phone rang, so Arthur hurried down the gloomy hallway. Hullo hullo, who is there?

It's me Arthur, a smooth low voice replied. It's Jack.

Jack? What a stroke of luck!

You left early so I rang to let you know that there's some urgent memos on your desk Arthur. I could drop them round if you like.

Really? That'd be wonderful.

Arthur was all at sea as he anticipated a visit from his secret lover. He guessed the family wouldn't be back for ages, giving him plenty of time alone with Jack to indulge himself.

Ah, Jack!

Arthur hung up the phone and stood for a moment lost in a trance. He gazed at his reflection in the heavy gilt mirror painted by May's great aunt Gertie. He saw his ageing face encircled by wattle and sprays of heather. His silver hair looked distinguished in the afternoon light and he smiled at his image held in the glass.

Arthur decided that he needed to freshen up before Jack arrived so he padded down the hall to the bathroom and ran some water into the basin. A quick dab of aftershave and a brush of his fine hair ensured that Arthur looked his best. He paused long enough at the sink for a last glance of his face before going back towards his bedroom.

What to wear puzzled Arthur?

He dumped his work clothes and pulled on a pair of casual grey cord trousers and a fresh shirt. Then Arthur donned his favourite smoking jacket with the embroidered patterns of dragons and chinese lettering. It was deep maroon with swirls of red and green and orange and it was by far Arthur's most desirable attire. He felt regal wearing the jacket, as though it put him where he belonged in the grand scheme of things.

Arthur was a victim of his own folly, a man of working-class stock who imagined himself above the average fellow.

But Jess knew better didn't she daddy dear?

Arthur poured himself a sherry from the handsome cedar cabinet in the dining room then lit a cigarette and waited. He was nervous and excited all at once, thinking only of Jack as he waited. Then suddenly the doorbell rang and there he was, the man of Arthur's dreams.

Come in come in, god you look so handsome!

The two men were soon in each other's arms as Arthur threw abandon to the wind. Before long he led Jack into the bedroom where they immediately threw themselves onto the marital bed with feverish intensity. Sighs and groans and terms of endearment were uttered between the two men as they writhed on the bed.

God you are so perfect Jack, yes yes yes!

The crumpled silk jacket lay abandoned on the bedroom floor along with a pile of assorted men's clothing. Jack and Arthur pulled up the covers and settled into each other with no thought for the outside world at all. It was as though there was no time in existence save their time.

Ah, this is bliss murmered Arthur.

How long they had lain there they did not know, but suddenly Arthur sensed they were no longer alone.

What what what? Who is that?

Jess had come back early because she'd been feeling sick all afternoon. May had put her on the bus and told her to go home to bed while she finished shopping with the others.

We won't be long dear, see you soon.

Jess had seen her father's car in the carport so she had gone round the back and quietly snuck in the back door so as not to disturb him. She knew that her father liked to read the paper and sip his sherry in peace in the afternoons. It was his habit to smoke and read and sip before dinner and woe betide the kids if they disturbed him. May would rebuke them sharply and give them extra chores.

So Jess didn't imagine that Arthur would be anywhere except in his favourite chair by the fire.

If I'm extra careful and quiet I might get to my room without father noticing I'm home.

On her way past Arthur's room Jess heard the briefest of noises coming from within.

That's funny, why would daddy be in there and who is he talking to?

She crept up and put her ear to the door before deciding boldly to peep in to her parent's bedroom. Quietly she opened the door just enough to take in the scene in her father's bed. Jess was puzzled at what she saw.

Nononono! What are you doing daddy? Who is that person with you?

Jess fled down the hallway to the safety of the back porch.

Had her father seen her she wondered?

Her breath was choking her and tears smarted her eyes as she curled herself tight into the soft fabric of the worn couch. She pulled an old blanket around her and shivered, not knowing or caring what to do next. It was too much really for her to take in. Jess didn't understand what was happening in that bed but she sure didn't want any part of it.

Did May have any idea what her husband was doing?

After a little while Jess heard the sound of an engine reversing back down the driveway. It faded into nothing and joined the highway din. Silence.

Has that man gone daddy? Has he?

By her own admission Jess was a news-aholic, so it was no surprise that she was intrigued by the current headlines. A large bulk coal carrier had run aground during a gale in Newcastle and was stuck fast on Nobbies beach.

Coals to Newcastle May had always said.

But Jess figured even May would have been surprised at the sight of the huge steel imposter which hunched on the shoreline of her favourite beach. The sand where Jess herself had spent her first seven summers splashing in the shallows. It was just too much.

Jess had learned the vagaries of the weather and the treachery of the sea from an early age.

Hadn't May told Jess that her great grandfather Joseph had drowned with his ship in those same waters so many years before?

As Jess watched the scene on the beach unfold now on her television set it brought back the memories submerged from her own childhood on Nobbies beach.

Can we go down to the beach today mummy, can we can we please?

Her mind flashed back to a kaleidoscope of sun-baked images which tumbled and tripped over each other in the haze of her mind. Jess could see her sisters clearly as they ran along the shoreline away from her.

Come back come back!

Jess racked her brain now for the information May had imparted about her forefathers in Newcastle. She looked at the huge steel ship on the screen before her and mentally compared it to the sixty one tonne wooden schooner her great grandfather Joseph had sailed up and down the coast.

Who would have thought, he would have muttered through his beard?

Joseph had been sailing back down the coast to reach Newcastle for the birth of his second child when his ship went down in a gale with the loss of all hands. May said it had happened in sight of the Newcastle

Heads but Jess knew that was only conjecture and that it was most likely further north. Whatever had happened the result was that May's grandmother was abruptly left a widow and her son never knew his own father who drowned before laying eyes on him.

Another disaster that's for sure thought Jess!

The only remaining relic of Joseph's sailing days was a boomerang that somehow landed on the deck of his ship up in the Richmond river on one of his trading runs. It was still in the family but fortunately not with Jess. She knew that having such a possession would bring bad luck and wanted none of it.

Well it sure has worked with our clan Jess mused and that's the truth so help me god!

Boomerangs are supposed to return . . . aren't they?

Jess opens the wooden shutters to let in the early morning light. It is a grey wintry day and the cold seeps through her ageing bones.

She goes to the sink and fills the kettle, placing it on the stove before heading out the back door to gather some kindling for the fire.

Back inside Jess bends down to set the fire as the kettle hums away behind her.

I'm coming Jess calls out, stop whistling at me!

That's the only thing that does *whistle at you these days dear . . . hahaha.*

The fire springs to life and Jess is instantly warmed.

Ah, that's good.

Jess squats there on the mat and gazes into the dancing flames, mesmerised. Her mind goes back to other fires in other places.

Heat for country cottages and seaside villas. Bonfires of her childhood. Camping and outdoor fires. Warm hearths in old English pubs. Burning leaves in Autumn. Bushfires hanging over the valley. Backburns at Easter. Footy barbecues every year for the grand final. Bush barbecues to collect firewood. Burning the rubbish in the Kimberly in the old 44 gallon drums. Flames against the black skies of Jess's childhood on Guy Fawkes night.

Jess laughs to herself at the recollections.

We don't do most of those things now of course it's simply not pc is it?

Now of course there are laws about caring for the environment and Jess is sure that's a good thing but it takes away most of the joy and the fun. *Doesn't it?*

Jess recalls the pleasure of watching the curls of smoke drift up into the sky on cold autumn days as the fires crackled and danced in the street. The piles of raked leaves would gather along the nature strips and sit in the gutters till they set the match to them. The children would leap and holler as the smoke eddied round them there in the dying afternoons. Their squeals of delight could be heard around the neighbourhood as they leaned on their rakes and surveyed a clean yard and were satisfied with a job well done.

But now Jess piles the remnant leaves and garden waste into large green bins made of plastic before dragging them out once a fortnight for the large greenwaste trucks that scour the neighbourhood in the pre-dawn light. They lumber along the street using enormous amounts of fuel to get the job done and Jess supposes it is progress, but really she is not so sure. *It's hardly the same, is it?*

When Jess sat down at the AA meeting she avoided everyone's gaze and tried to stay calm. Part of her knew that she shouldn't really be there, but she stayed anyway. She had to, Bert was going to drive her home.

Welcome welcome, Jess heard someone say. We'll start off with the usual, alright? And tonight we have a new person at our meeting. Welcome Jess, we'll each say a little then it will be your turn. Alright?

Help!

Jess tries to focus on their words but her brain is in melt-down.

Hullo my name is Lyn and I'm an alcoholic. This week I stayed away from the hotel and it's now been three weeks since I had a drink.

Hullo my name is Jim and I'm an alcoholic. I haven't been near the RSL for two months. It's been a struggle but I feel like I'm getting there.

Hullo my name is Jess and I'm . . . . *help!*

Jess can't say it, she's *not* an alcoholic.

Am I?

Jess looks down in shame. These people are so giving and so friendly and so *normal.* And that's what hits her all of a sudden. There are teachers and a doctor and priest and businessmen. How could this be?

Jess feels a sense of hopelessness wash over her but it is mixed with the beginning of some sort of acceptance as well. She knows she is here for a reason so she'd better get her act together and work out what she needs to do.

I can't open up to this group of strangers, I just can't!

The meeting continues but Jess is in denial and withdraws into herself.

She feels defiant and a little bit angry. Not at *them,* at herself for letting things get to this point.

I should have done something sooner about my drinking.

A *lot* sooner. But at least Jess is finally starting to figure it out and do something about it.

Isn't she?

Bree and Jess get their scooters out of the garage and ride down to their favourite café. It is a June Sunday morning and the air is cold as they manoeuvre through the traffic. When they stop at the lights Jess calls out to Bree, geez are you cold?

Damn right, Bree replies, I've got tears in my eyes!

They laugh at each other as the lights change to green.

Oh well the bikes needed a run Jess yells, just as well we're not going too far.

They reach the city and park near the café.

Shit I'm sure glad to get off the bike says Bree. Let's get inside where it's warm.

The café is unusually quiet this morning with noone seated outside. Normally at this time on a Sunday it's packed with breakfast-goers.

It must be the miserable weather says Bree. Everyone must have decided to stay home. Oh well.

They place their orders for coffee then go out the back to their usual spot. The fire is going in the old chimney so Bree and Jess huddle close and stretch their hands out to warm up.

I love this place says Bree. It's just us isn't it?

Sure is replies Jess. What a find eh?

They smile at each other and giggle like a couple of kids. It feels to Jess as though the two of them are on an adventure, but the best part is that it always feels like this when they are together.

How lucky are we? Lucky lucky.

Sometimes we make our own luck and sometimes it just falls out of the sky Jess thinks. Take my meeting Bree for example, who would've guessed that she'd move into the apartment next door when I least expected it? Go figure.

Some things are meant to happen and some things aren't.

Being with Bree was fate and Jess never questioned that for one moment.

But not all luck is good luck and didn't Jess just know it. When things go well and you don't drop any stitches in the knitting it's great Jess surmised, but sometimes the stitches in your life just drop off of their own accord and there doesn't seem to be much you can do about it.

That's just how it was when Paul died. What the hell do you do when it's so sudden and unexpected? It was so damned hard to pick up the stitches wasn't it?

The day after Paul's sudden death the family had gathered for Christmas more with sadness at the getting together than joy. They hadn't even had time to arrange the funeral. It was too soon.

And besides, it was a public holiday, another bloody disaster!

The family tried to break through their sorrow and numbness but they were all too brittle and the grief was too raw, it hung over them like a drooling vulture gripping them in it's talons. Snatches of smiles broke through from time to time but mostly there was silence. They tried not to talk about it of course. The death. So recent. Paul. *Paulllll!*

The tree where the presents had been bunched together in family groups stood silently as sentinel guarding the family grief. It seemed gaudy and inept under the circumstances, as though somehow it was an imposter without the presence of Paul.

The children were filled with the expectation of the opening of presents of course, but the adults mourned and delayed the ritual for a time. Hoping maybe that it wasn't true. That Paul wasn't really gone. That perhaps after all there'd been some horrible mistake and he'd suddenly appear and join them after all for the Christmas celebration.

Of course it didn't happen.

Jess had glanced across at the small piles of gifts till she noticed Paul's. They were wrapped in bright colors and tied with bows and holly. They left them there of course, under the tree.

He'll never get them now . . . will he?

The presents were a symbol of something that was and could have been but wouldn't ever be again, a life now extinguished.

But the little children were impatient with the waiting so the festivities finally began.

They were so young and eager and didn't understand the loss. It was the adults who did the suffering.

Here this one's yours here you are said James as he acted out the Santa role. Look look. Come and open this and see what santa has brought you. Aren't you lucky?

But Paul wasn't so lucky.

Jess had felt the anger rising again despite the festive occasion. Despite the gathering of the family.

We'd all let Paul down. Hadn't we?

For Jess's thirteenth birthday May and Arthur gave her a brand new riding helmet. It was navy blue velvet with a satin ribbon at the back and Jess thought it was the most wonderful present she'd ever received.

She had already acquired a pair of second hand riding boots and jodhpurs along the way, so now she had a complete riding outfit and she was thrilled.

But of course she didn't have a horse and had long since given up asking.

During the week Jess would still sit on the back fence and watch the dairy horses, and on weekends she rode her bike for miles out to nearby farms where they kept horses.

Occasionally Jess would pass a gymkhana in progress and she would pedal in on her bike and hang around there for hours hoping to get a ride.

She watched girls her age compete in jumping and dressage events on beautiful well-groomed horses. Jess was very envious and she felt sure that she could do as well if only she had her own horse.

I could, I know I could!

Another disaster wasn't it?

Jess knew that Arthur and May never really understood her desire for a horse, and maybe it wouldn't have mattered even if they had.

Jess and her own small family went home after Paul's funeral, back to the country town where they lived. Back to their world and friends and their lives a long way away from Jess's family.

But in truth she'd been a long way apart from family right from the beginning in the brick house in Newcastle.

I should have been there for Paul, Jess wailed to her husband, and now it's too late and I can't fix it can I?

It's not your fault he replied, it's not anybody's fault. It's just one of those things that happen you know.

But Jess *didn't* know, and that was the trouble. She didn't *want* to know. It just wasn't *right*.

Of course it wasn't Jess's first experience with death in the family, Arthur had already gone. But at least he'd been sixty four and not twenty one. At least he'd lived a lot more of his life, hadn't he?

But Paul was so young Jess said to her husband, so young. It's just not fair! He had all his life ahead of him and now it's gone.

Gone. Gonegonegonegone . . . .

Jess tried of course to find reasons but she struggled. She couldn't make sense of any of it, especially the argument at May's house the afternoon before he died. Jess sure didn't want to think about that, it made her too angry.

Way too angry!

Jess sure as hell didn't want to drop any more stitches.

Have you ever looked through a kaleidoscope and been totally fascinated by the myriad of colored patterns reflected Jess one blustery September afternoon? That's what life can be like when the knitting is going well. When there are no disasters and dropped stitches, nothing but smooth sailing with maybe a couple of unexpected wind changes along the way.

There were lots of those times for Jess. Colored patterns and plain sailing. Fun. Warmth and sharing and happiness.

But they came to me later after I'd left the family home, didn't they?

The first thing Jess did after her Graduation was move as far away from home as she could. Still within the state boundary of course, but only just. North East country. Hills and valleys and snow and rivers. Creeks and waterholes for fishing and swimming. Snow to ski on in winter. Wide open spaces and tree-covered hills to ride horses at breakneck speed.

Jess loved her new sense of freedom and abandonement.

Lucky lucky.

Jess felt a new beginning and she savoured every minute of it. She bought a motor bike and sought adventure. She made new friends.

She finally belonged somewhere.

They travelled all over the place at weekends. Country pubs, ski fields, lakes, rivers, theatres, shops. On a dare one night they even drove all the way to Melbourne for a hamburger then slept on the beach. It took six hours to get there. Jess loved it all.

And the strange thing was that we all paired up and eventually married, how did that happen?

Looking back Jess guessed it was just one of those things. Small country town, happens all the time.

And down the track all these years later they all still have occasional contact. Some are still married but not Jess.

We divorced years ago.

Hannah is not home much when Jess begins her teenage years. She is *out*.

Mother says dear dear and tut tut and father shakes his head and smiles resignedly as he sips his nightly sherry.

Whatever is the matter dear and why are you worrying so he asks May? She's a good girl Hannah and she'll be alright you'll see.

But mother saw alright, and she didn't like it at all. Arthur was rarely involved in the day to day lives of his growing offspring, and that left most of the work to May.

As usual.

May knew that Hannah had started seeing boys and she was nervous and uncomfortable about it, but there was little she could do to reel her oldest daughter in. Hannah lived by her own rules, always had and always would. She'd never listened much to May and she sure wasn't going to start now. Not when life was so full of promise and adventure.

And *boys*.

The children were all at school or working now and May felt abandoned and slightly adrift. Arthur would chide her when she complained of feeling neglected but she felt it nonetheless. He had a role in the outside world which had passed her by, and she desperately needed to redress the situation somehow at this stage of her life.

May was in her fifties when she announced to Arthur quite boldly one evening that she wanted a job outside the family home.

Whatever are you thinking my dear, Arthur asked incredulously? What will people think, that I am unable to provide for my family? No dear, it simply won't do. I won't have you working, and besides May, what could you possibly do that is more important than taking care of *us*?

May simpered and withdrew for a time but then rallied once more. She secretly sought work until she was successful in landing a job with a local real estate agent as a secretary. May had learned shorthand and typing over the years and now wanted to put these skills to better use. After all she surmised, the family would be just fine during the daytime without spending all her spare time on unnecessary chores wouldn't they?

And really they don't need me here cosseting them now, even the baby Paul, do they?

So May persisted in following her desire of a belated career despite Arthur's opposition. She'd earned her independence, hadn't she?

Jess was a late bloomer when it came to dating and boys and all that stuff, it just didn't appeal to her.

But it wasn't that way for her sisters, especially Hannah. Jess could hardly blame her for wanting to spread her wings a little and get out of the house as often as she could.

I know how you feel Hannah . . . trapped.

Jess was only thirteen when Hannah was married and it happened all in a rush. The ceremony took place in the family loungeroom and it was a very small wedding. Jess didn't really recall much of it to tell the truth. It didn't mean much to her at the time except that Hannah would no longer be living at home. And *that* was a blessing, Jess finally got her own bedroom.

Thank you thank you wedding god.

But Jess knew that the wedding was more about necessity than celebration. Hannah was pregnant, and May and Arthur were not amused. The groom's parents were far from happy too, and there were quite a few heated words exchanged at the time.

But they failed to make any sense to Jess, who just drifted through it all alone as usual. There was nothing she could do to save Hannah anyway, it was too late for that wasn't it?

But the really strange thing is that of all the pairings Hannah's was the only one to survive throughout the years.

They are still together. Go figure.

At high school Jess made new friends. Not many, but enough to keep her buoyed throughout the teen years.

Jess became increasingly assertive and popular and developed an outgoing nature unlike her introverted behaviour at home. She became the class spokesperson and clown and as a result was often in trouble at school.

Jess was pretty testy in those early years at high school, but eventually must have settled a bit and developed some responsibility. She played team sports and was elected captain several times. She represented the school at swimming carnivals, and as a matter of course became both house captain and prefect. The shy and lonely child had apparently disappeared.

Jess supposed her parents were proud of her in their own way for those achievements but they never showed it. She never really *felt* their acceptance or admiration. It was always ephemeral and intangible, lurking in the background somewhere. But Jess had already learned to do without it long before high school so it didn't have much impact by then.

But still it hurt.

The beach was still the centre of Jess's existence in those erratic teenage years. The sand and the sea. Toasting bodies in skimpy bikinis at The Fernery.

Splashing in the shallows or swimming out to the end of the pier. Laughing and gossiping and eying off the boys. Pushing and shoving each other and shouting as Jess and her friends ran over the hot sand to be first in the water.

Sun glorious sun. And freedom.

But of course it was freedom with rules even though Jess didn't recognise that at the time. She was too busy having fun to realise that she was still dropping stitches in the knitting.

And boy did I have trouble picking up those stitches sometimes.

The rules of teenagers were many and varied and they changed constantly. Jess should have known, she'd grown up with Hannah after all.

But when it's *you* that's in the middle of the teen thing somehow it's very different, isn't it Jess pondered? It pays to listen and watch for a while before you join the game, at least that's what she quickly discovered. The rules are never written and barely spoken either, they just *are*.

And somehow you have to pick them up and run with them and let them become part of your world if you want to survive.

At least that's what Jess discovered when she stepped into the alien world of puberty all those years ago.

Jess was lucky because she was a fast learner. She'd had to be in her family, that's was how it was.

So Jess picked up most of the teen rules whether they were out there or not and she adapted them to suit herself, keeping what she *really* thought to herself. She developed the accepted behaviour codes of the gang and joined in to play the game and adopt the cloak of membership.

But they weren't really a gang at all, just a bunch of kids from mainly middle class families trying to establish themselves. They were building the access bridge into the adult world step by step, tentatively stomping through the murkiness of adolescence.

To Jess it felt like stretching the boundaries of who they were and who they thought they should be if only their parents wouldn't object. They were small time really, hemmed in by convention despite their weak attempts at rebellion from time to time.

But that didn't stop us did it?

Jess finds it hard to believe that in a matter of months she will become a grandma. How could that be? What has happened to all those years in between?

Jess laughs silently to herself as she sits in the kitchen with her feet propped on the hearth sipping another cup of tea.

She is wrapped in the old terry towelling dressing gown with her daggy old felt slippers on.

I must look like a grandma, heeelp!

Secretly of course Jess is delighted and she doesn't really mind at all. The reality of becoming a grandma is just so damn *exciting!*

Two of Jess's friends are also having grandchildren this year and Jess tells them they should form a grandma club and get together every month for coffee and to compare notes.

What a hoot they say. Yes let's, it'll be fun.

They laugh together and smile above their double chins, ignoring the wrinkled faces and grey hair.

Bugger it, we're still young, aren't we?

May is insistent about the job as secretary but Arthur is having none of it.

No wife of mine is going to work he shouts and that's final!

May retreats for a while and shuts herself in the bedroom.

Not again!

She feels the flush of defeat as she crumples temporarily onto the marital bed. A draft creeps through under the doorway but it is the draft that rolls through the corridors of her brain that chills May and renders her mute.

It's not fair, it's not she sobs.

Jess used to think it was a waste of time measuring life but not any more. She is a creature of habit, so every day Jess rations small portions of her existence.

Too many years of timetables and bells I suppose.

Routine and structure, that's what her life has become.

Sounds dead boring I know but in a funny way it nurtures me.

Jess needs a framework for her days now that she is no longer working full time.

Knit one purl one knit one . . . .

Her days are still fairly structured despite the fact that Jess mainly works at home in the office. Her routine is probably repetitive and pretty bland but it keeps Jess going and she loves the solitariness and creativity.

She is still held captive by the words.

Thank you word god thank you.

There are mundane aspects of her life to attend to of course but Jess doesn't mind. Walks, washing, dishes, sweeping, phone calls, bills, mail, folding, sorting. All the stuff that never goes away no matter what.

May used to say she never bothered with the dusting any more when she was old and white haired and in decline.

It never grows past a certain height any way, so why bother cleaning?

Jess used to laugh, May had a point she supposed but the place looked shabby and dirty and dreadfully unkempt in the end. But May didn't care, she'd just shrug it off and spend most of her time out doors in her beloved garden anyway. That's just the way she was and who could blame her?

It was easier for May to ignore the daily grime with her fading eyesight so that's just what she did. Jess figured that her mother had already spent enough hours of her life cleaning and scrubbing and taking care of others so now it didn't matter any more. May only had herself to worry about now and that was that. She didn't feel the need to justify it to anyone.

But Jess was different, she liked order and neatness.

Always have. Maybe it's a control thing left over from my childhood in the brick house on the hill.

Deep down Jess knew that it was related to declaring her own space and taking care of it and keeping it safe away from Hannah and Ruby and James.

Don't go there Jess, not today!

Or maybe more than a part of it was down to Jess's genes despite the denial. Arthur and his sister Maud were the tidy and organised ones in the family and didn't Jess just know it? She knew it was the English blood and not the Australian, but she wished now that she had more time with her parents to discover such things.

May always said you need a sense of humour in this life, but there wasn't much of either in Jess's childhood. Sense *or* Humour.

Not that I'm complaining. I discovered laughter later on. Lucky me.

As for May, well there wasn't much in her life to give her joy was there?

Take the career disaster when May sure was left out in the cold.

After her weak attempts to convince Arthur that she really could work outside the home she withdrew to the confines of her bedroom where she stayed for the best part of a week. Her head was heavy with the defeat meted out by her husband, and May felt the final insult of unworthiness in Arthur's dismissal. She lay silent and contrite on the marital bed with the blinds drawn, secretly hoping that some of her smouldering anger and ill-will would transfer to Arthur and cause him the anguish he deserved. Her confidence which had so recently been buoyed by the opportunity to prove herself worthy in the outside world was once again dashed on the rocky shoreline of failure. May was sinking beneath the foam as she abandoned all hope of rescue.

Harold oh Harold, where are you now?

As each new day dawned May regained tiny portions of her former strength but it was not enough this time.

So Jess found it not entirely surprising that she rarely saw May laugh.

If there was any comedy and lightness in her life she must have learned to keep it all inside and Jess understood that.

Maybe that's why she spent so many hours wandering round her garden over the years in search of happiness or inner peace.

Or whatever came close to it for May.

Of course there were moments Jess remembered when a smile crossed May's face and she seemed happy, but they were few and far between. At least that's how Jess recalls it in her later years.

May had her own demons and doubts and worries to deal with as well as all the practical stuff over the years. She never really opened up to Jess and maybe it was because she never quite forgave her for the difficult birth.

I don't know.

There were so many reasons May had to hold a grudge and Jess was probably the least of them when all's said and done. Blame her own mother for favouring the sons and not the daughter. Blame Arthur for all his absences. Blame the Depression for delaying the wedding. Blame the war for rationing. Blame her husband and mother for the loss of the first baby. Blame nursing for catching dyptheria. Blame the brothers for becoming doctors when she was only a nurse.

Blame the five children for causing such mess and upset in her life.

Let's face it when it came to the blame god May could have a field day.

Jess assumed it was the way May looked at things that caused so much greyness in her life. She let things get so *serious* didn't she?

Take it easy mum Jess used to think.

Even as a child Jess could see the clouds gathering behind May's furrowed brow, and puzzled why she was like that. Why May couldn't see the lighter side of things. Why she had to make such hard work of it all the time. It seemed so futile and wasted to Jess.

Geez mum take it easy will you life's not all that bad you know I wanted to yell at her. But of course I didn't, not when I was young.

Jess kept it all inside because that's what she'd learnt to do.

Stiff upper lip dear and don't you just know it. For King and country.

Crap. Bugger bum. Bloody hell.

Jess hated May's stupid sayings as she grew older, but of course she didn't say it aloud. May hated swearing or crassness.

Bugger bugger bugger!

May would go ballistic! We don't use that language in this house Jess you know that go to your room.

But later when I finally rebelled I let it out, didn't I?

The sun has finally broken through the fog. It is shining through Jess's office window and drawing her outside.

Mack barks in the back yard as Jess hears the washing machine grind to a halt. The tradies have arrived next door and are starting up their machines. Neighbourhood noises distract Jess but she doesn't mind this morning.

Some time today they are replacing the back fence so Jess is going into the city to meet Bree for coffee. It's not too cold today so Jess decides to walk.

It'll do me good, I need the exercise.

That's another thing about ageing isn't it Jess thinks, the changing body shape?

Oh yes, you'd better believe it! Hahaha.

Jess remembers when she was a size 14. Once she spent most of her summers in a bikini at the beach and thought nothing of it, Jess had terrific legs and a stomach that was tanned and as flat as an ironing board. True! But what the hell? Who needs an ironing board these days anyway laughed Jess? Noone irons any more.

Jess smiles to herself at the irony of it all. She no longer cares about size and shape of course, what's the point?

Jess isn't as bad as May though, she hasn't removed all the mirrors in the house. Jess just doesn't look in them as much as she used to.

Haven't for ages really and that's the honest truth. Vanity is definitely for the young, they need it. I don't.

In San Fransisco Jess and Bree walk and walk. Up the hills and down the other side. Jess laughs at herself as she recalls the childhood songs.

The grand old Duke of York . . . .

Bugger me, Jess says to Bree, we're just like those troops aren't we? Marching up hill and down dale, but I'll bet they were a bit fitter than us. I sure as hell hope so or they'd never have got to the battle would they?

They are at the top of Nob Hill and the view of the bay is great.

Look look they shout aloud, isn't that grand?

A cable car comes along so Bree and Jess jump on and stand on the running board as it descends towards China Town. They wave and hoot and shout at passers by like a couple of madwomen.

Anyone would think we were Aussies fair dinkum they would Jess shouts at Bree. Hahaha.

We are having such fun.

The tram stops and they get off at China Town. Immediately they feel at home as they are folded into the sights and smells and bustle of the crowded street.

Just like parts of Melbourne isn't it Bree yells above the street din as they cross the road?

Bree wants to look at jade but Jess want to look at baby clothes for the new grandchild. There are so many market stalls and small dingy shops stacked full of Asian goods.

It's our kind of world.

Bree and Jess lose themselves in the joy and clutter and clamour of it all. They are in heaven.

That night back at the hotel Jess tries to call her daughter on her mobile in central Australia where she is working till the next ski season.

Lucky lucky.

First Jess tries to dial out on the hotel phone without success. She's sure she has the right code for Australia, so Jess phones the hotel lobby and asks them how to make the call.

You can't do it from your room they say. Come down to the desk and we'll help you.

Damn, Jess thinks, I don't want to go out.

Down at the desk Jess is assisted by the young clerk who is on duty at the time. At first they can't connect the number so the clerk tries a few different combinations of the international dial code. Drop the 1. Add a 0. Is that 01 or just 1? What area code do you need? Jess explains that she is calling a mobile but the clerk insists there should be more numbers.

After several unsuccessful attempts they call the operator, who suggests Jess should buy a phone card as it will be cheaper to call from a pay phone. The clerk tells Jess she can get one across the road and that there is a pay phone at the Laundromat.

Jess returns to her room to get some money and tells Bree what she's doing. It's now been half an hour since she first tried to phone and Jess is getting pissed off.

Bloody international phone god! See what I mean about technology?

Jess is finally at the pay phone with her card but it won't connect.

Of course.

She dials the operator again who replies, no you can't use that card for a mobile number in Australia.

Give me strength I think. Lordy lordy!

At last the operator finally gives Jess the correct code and says to call from the hotel desk. That's the best way she says.

Aaaagh!

It's now over an hour since Jess first attempted the call to Australia and she is getting mighty hot under the collar.

Isn't this supposed to be the almighty U S of A? Why can't I even make a simple call to Australia then?

Finally Jess hears her daughter's voice on the phone clear as a bell, and she laughs aloud if a little hysterically down the line.

What's happening mumsie, her daughter asks? How're things going over there?

Hahaha. Bloody great I say. They've got the best of everything here kiddo, especially their phones. Goddamn marvellous!

How are things with you anyway Jess asks? How's the Rock these days?

Can't complain the girl answers.

Bloody oath Jess responds, noone would listen anyway kiddo, especially the phone gods. They don't listen to anyone. Hahaha.

But her daughter doesn't understand what Jess is babbling on about. *Probably thinks I'm becoming a little unhinged or time warped or something. Hahaha.*

Okay mum I'd better go I've got to get to work she says. Bye for now.

Jess replaces the phone with a sigh and wonders aloud what that was all about?

Who knows says Bree, perhaps the AAPT gods don't work in Oz!

Jess collapses onto the bed with a wry grin in Bree's direction. Bugger it anyway, let's go down to the pool for a swim before tea.

Not me says Bree, you go on ahead if you like. I'm stuck on this American tv show at the moment and don't you just love the ads they have here Jess?

This product may cause dizzy spells and headaches see your doctor if . . .

Geez I know what they mean guffaws Jess as she races downstairs!

It's the day of May's funeral and Jess is not sure how she feels. Coping well outwardly but what about the inner Jess? It was a sudden death after all and she's still adjusting isn't she?

James just left a message on my phone when she died.

I can't believe it Bree says, how could he do that to you?

Well that's my family Jess replies. Caring aren't they? Hahaha.

They congregate in the foyer of the funeral parlour for the usual nodding of heads and forced smiles.

I'm over it, I think. Piss off!

They file into the chapel where Bree and Jess sit in the second row. Jess hates being too obvious.

No need to make a statement now is there. Not for May anyway, she's dead. And I'm buggered if I want to make a statement for the living.

Ruby saunters in with her brood and takes up the front row of course.

As though she is the favoured one.

At least that's what Jess thinks, it's not half obvious. Ruby sniffles into a tissue and looks around with a subdued grin as if to tell the rest of them that they are inferior somehow. She acts as though she was the only one that cared about mother but Jess knows differently.

She's a user. A pretender. A fraud.

Jess ignores Ruby's theatrics and focuses on the coffin, which takes centre stage of course.

It's the dead that take over here, not the living. Haha Ruby.

Jess's mind is a maelstrom of memories, and she tries not to think of the body in the box as her mother. She'd been to see her and said her farewell alone.

Talk about life imitating art.

Jess is stuck in the past, on who May was as a person.

As my mother.

She sees May smiling on the beach as they play on the sand and taking her brood for Saturday bus rides. Shopping, gardening, sewing, cooking, playing her beloved piano, drinking endless cups of tea. May in her nurse's uniform in the old sepia photos. May with Arthur. Her parents.

But something is stuck somewhere, something is missing. What?

Emotion. *Feeling.* How could that be?

What is Jess *really* thinking and feeling as she stares fixedly at May's coffin? Why don't the tears come? Why does she feel so detached from the ritual of the funeral?

Why do I just seem to be an observer?

Jess glances across at the others. James and his family. Ruby and her boys.

And of course Hannah is there. Hannah and her husband and children.

Wouldn't you just know it? Dressed to the nines and all tight smiles and frowns and decorum. Look at me look at me, Hannah's countenance beckons!

Paul is not here of course to farewell his mother.

He left before her, didn't he?

But Jess doesn't want to think about that today nor about the other family funerals. Arthur. Paul. And now May, her mother.

Jess is suddenly overtaken by sadness and emptiness but it is not for her. It is for what might have been, not what *was*.

I'm having a senior's moment Jess yells at Bree from the kitchen. I came in here for something and I've forgotten what it was.

Christ don't you just hate that Bree replies and they squeal with laughter.

Bugger, say Jess between giggles, the age god is playing up again. Haha.

Now what *was* it I wanted to find? Sounds like . . . . bugger, I've lost it.

Ah well, now that I'm here I'll put the kettle on, sighs Jess.

Would you like a cuppa dear she asks Bree?

Is the Pope catholic she replies?

Then Jess remembers what it was.

I got an email back from that place in Saxilby, she tells Bree. You know, the one I sent to the pub where grandma used to live when she was a little girl. Remember we went there on our trip? The Sun Inn.

Fancy that says Bree, the wonders of modern technology!

Don't start, I reply. Bloody technology gods! Hahaha. Pass the sugar will you dear? Ta. What are you doing today?

Don't know yet, I might go downtown and cruise the shops for a bit replies Bree, how about you? Are you doing more writing dear?

It feels like groundhog day Jess says casting a dark look Bree's way. You know how things are sometimes, maybe I'm having a whole goddamn senior's *day*, not just a moment. Damn!

There there Jess, Bree commiserates. Don't let it get to you, I'm sure you'll be just fine once you get back to your laptop.

Maybe we'll go for a drive down the coast road when I've finished today, how would that be, asks Jess?

I'm stuck in a time warp and I don't know why.

Perhaps it's all this dredging up the boggy sands of my childhood reflects Jess, digging and shovelling through the layers of her yesterdays.

She suddenly feels becalmed, stranded on the beaches of her past. Waiting and watching. Looking far out to sea.

What is it I am seeking?

A year after May's funeral Jess went to visit James. He had the ashes and Jess wanted them back so she could take May home.

Back to her roots. Back to Newcastle and her beloved sea.

Hi Curl how are ya? James greets Jess at the door in his usual daggy farm clothes. Want a cuppa?

Okay, there's something I want to talk to you about Jess blurts.

They sit out on the verandah in the weak winter sun and Jess asks her brother about May's ashes.

I've got them out there in a purple box he says, the funeral director gave them to me. Had them in the back of the car for a while he says. Geez the ol' girl did more travelling with me than that she did for quite a while when she was still living!

Hahahah.

James laughs into his coffee and lights up another cigarette. He coughs and splutters as Jess stares at him through the smoke haze. James is so thin these days and Jess can't help but notice his decline, he's not yet sixty but looks a lot older.

The age god seems to have sure done a number on James, lordy lordy!

May would like to go home Jess tells James, I know she would. I'll bet she'd love the trip.

The two siblings have a bit of a giggle but underneath there is still so much stuff unresolved isn't there?

And of course we never talk about it.

That's just the way it is.

James passes Jess the shiny purple plastic box containing the ashes and she holds it in her lap. It feels strange to have the last bit of anything physical here to connect with her mother, but the cynical part of her says don't be so damn stupid Jess, it's just ash, the same as you empty out of the fireplace dear. And besides, how do you know it's really May's? *Could be anybody's ash in there couldn't it?*

But Jess doesn't want to consider that possibility, it's too bizarre. So she sits there on the old wooden chair cradling the box on her knee and sips at the hot strong coffee.

I reckon she'd like that sis, James blurts out. You going up there then, to Newcastle?

Yes. I'm going up on her birthday next week Jess replies. It's what she'd want I'm sure. I'll take her back to the breakwater at Nobby's beach. *Home.*

May must have had music in her soul but most of the time you wouldn't have known it thought Jess. Maybe it was her welsh heritage, Jess didn't know.

May probably had tunes in her head that her children never heard, ditties and catches of songs. Music passed on from her folk.

It always seemed strange to Jess that the only music that filled her childhood home was from May's piano. It was played most days during the afternoon, at least that's how Jess recalls it anyhow.

May would hum tunes occasionally but Jess didn't know what they were. Not songs or nursery rhymes that Jess recognised or remembered. But there were a few tunes that they had learned as kids and sung around the piano with May. Silent Night at Christmas.

That's one I used to sing.

Doesn't Jess have a lovely voice dear she sings that so sweetly mother used to say to Arthur?

Yes dear it's lovely he'd reply through the smoke from his pipe, can you play that again dear?

Arthur had a couple of favourite songs which May would dutifully play for him. Old Man River and Begin the Beguine. He'd lean up against that old piano and sing away as though there were no tomorrows, and for a short moment in time Jess's parents would be connected as though they were held in each other's spell.

But those moments were rare, or that's how it seemed to Jess.

When I was the little sister many years ago.

Let's get the train to the city today dear what do you think, Jess says to Bree as they sip their morning coffee by the fire. We could drive to the station and catch the 8.45.

Bree smiles across at Jess and says yes let's. It'll be fun she says, just like running away for the day.

What a hoot Jess replies, but what are we running away from hahaha?

They laugh into their coffees and shove their feet onto the brick hearth to get warm. They are silent for a while just staring into the flames, then Bree breaks the silence.

Let's go over to St Kilda she says excitedly, we can go to that great op shop and Acland St. I love it over there she adds.

Yes yes Jess chips in. Let's do that then, we'll take the tram. It'll be fun won't it? We might see what's on at the George too and see a film if we have time, what do you think Bree?

We could wander through the city and go down Hardware Lane to all those outdoor cafes, replies Bree.

Later on the train Jess reads the paper for a while and does the crosswords, glancing around occasionally at the other passengers. Jess plays the guessing game again in her head, trying to match each person with their name and lifestyle and occupation.

She writes their stories in her head as she often does.

Maybe it is something that I started when I was the small white haired one in the brick house all those years ago.

The train pulls in to Southern Cross station.

It used to be called Spencer St but they changed it of course.

The station is being rebuilt and it's a mess of half-finished steel and plastic and concrete. Bits of paper are stuck to temporary fences with arrows pointing directions but passengers seem confused and Jess doesn't blame them. Still the rush continues.

Let's get the train to Flinders St station, Jess calls out to Bree as they begin the long march along the platform.

Great, says Bree, but how do we get there?

I'll ask someone Jess yells above the din, that's the easiest way.

Platform 3 the attendant says and points to the escalator. Up there and turn left. Next train departs in a few minutes.

Thanks Jess says as they head for the escalator, what a mess! Goodness knows what visitors to the city think about all this.

Well I'm sure it will look terrific when it's all finished says Bree optimistically. Hope so anyway.

I have my doubts Jess strains above the din as they descend the escalator to platform three, we'll wait and see.

The train is about to depart so Bree and Jess hop on and find a seat near the door. It is one of the new trains full of shiny plastic and bright colors.

Better than the old red rattlers I used to travel on to College in the sixties Jess hollers to Bree, they were shockers. Draughty and noisy as hell, full of body heat and smoke and sighs and shouts and litter and old newspapers and cigarette butts, at least that's how I remember them.

In my third year I spent two hours a day in the damn things Jess hoots, then there was the long walk up Swanston St to the uni. Used to pass the old Carlton Brewery, god it stank Bree protests. Bloody long walk that was and I was always carrying heaps of art student stuff wasn't I?

One day I decided to get a tram down to Flinders St from Carlton adds Jess. I couldn't really afford it but I was carrying a large awkward painting so I got the tram at the uni stop, but blow me down if the conductor didn't charge me an extra fare for the painting!

Be damned I said, it's not a person, anyone can see that can't they? Jess guffaws at the memory and Bree glances at her strangely as their train rattles through the city loop.

So what happened Bree asks?

Well the conductor replied that's bad luck dear but it's policy, the painting is taking up too much room so you'll have to pay or get off the tram.

Jess had looked him in the eye and tried to outwit him but it was a lost cause and didn't she know it?

Bloody bureaucracy gone mad she fumes, I'd like to hit him.

But she didn't, where would that get her after all?

Bloody nowhere, that's where.

The trammie by now has a sarcastic grin on his face and is waiting for my money Jess tells Bree as she continues the story, he knows he is winning and I think it's a game he plays with the students. A power trip thing. *Look at me in my uniform I win hahaha!*

So Jess paid the extra fare and shuffled across to stand in the doorway where she leant the painting against the side of the tram.

Just for fun I began to talk to the painting to annoy the trammie, Jess recalls. I figure that seeing he made me pay a fare for this piece of wood and canvas I'll treat it as a person, hahaha.

Bree looks at Jess aghast then roars with laughter at the mental image Jess conjures up from the past. Well don't start talking to your backpack now will you Bree shrieks, or I'm getting off this train at the next goddamn stop so help me!

The other passengers on the tram laughed at Jess realising it's all a bit of entertainment. Which it was

Jess supposed, but later she realised how silly she must have looked.

It's a wonder they didn't drag me off and lock me up! Lordy lordy.

Bree laughs aloud at the story as their train pulls into the station.

God you're such a dag Jess she says, trust you to talk to a damn painting on a tram. No wonder people were staring at you at the time. Hahaha.

Let's go over to Fed Square and have a look around Jess says as they wait at the lights on Swanston St. Might as well have a coffee while we're there in one of those new cafes, what do you think Bree?

Sounds good to me!

The cleaners are finishing up after the early morning soccer festivities and Jess thinks that it's just as well the Socceroos got a draw.

At least we go into the next round at the world cup Jess tells Bree as they cross the patterned brickwork to a café, with the way those umpires were working it would have been a bloody riot over there if we'd lost. I reckon the Aussies would have stormed the field too right they would have!

You've got a point there replies Bree, it doesn't bear thinking about. Bloody umpires, they're worse than over here she says. At least with Aussie rules we know the deal! Bloody football they laugh, hahaha.

There was no football in Jess's life when she was the little sister.

That came later when I was free.

Jess looks back with amazement at her barren childhood, wondering why she is now so interested in sport.

Not because of Arthur and May that's for sure!

Arthur had shown an occasional interest in the cricket, but Jess realises it was the elitism that drew him in.

Of course, it was the English thing to do wasn't it?

Later on Arthur played the occasional friendly game of cricket with colleagues but it certainly wasn't a part of the family fabric, not at all.

Jess wished it had been, she'd needed some healthy diversions in her formative years.

So Jess took it upon herself to branch out and become a team player when she reached high school. She was a natural swimmer so that was easy. Jess swam for her school house every year as well as for the school in inter school competitions. Winning came easily despite the lack of any sort of training program in Jess's life. None of the kids Jess knew had even heard of training for competition, much less having a coach to help. It wasn't an option.

Hannah and Jess inherited Arthur's sense of occasion and attention to detail. Ruby and James and Paul definitely missed out there.

Mind you, the detail thing might have come from May who was pretty organised in her own way.

But the importance of the moment was definitely Arthur's trait, not that they saw much of it at home because he didn't bother too much with his offspring. The children were mainly left to May, Arthur had other far more important duties to occupy his time didn't he?

Yes yes you did didn't you . . . daddy dear?

Arthur was sitting in his office lost in thought. He scanned the room slowly, taking in it's grandeur. It was his domain and he loved it.

More than he loved going home most nights.

His eyes rested on the magnificent sideboard which stood three metres tall. It was made of cedar and intricately-carved with faces and scenes of the early history of settlement in his adopted country, and Arthur never ceased to be impressed with it's detail.

There were other pieces of furniture too, but the large sideboard was by far Arthur's favourite and he relished the prospect of showing it off to newcomers in his office. He boasted that it was an original owned by the family who had built the large seaside mansion, and as such could probably be traced back to the late nineteenth century. That pleased Arthur with his sense of the importance of the historical, and he felt it gave him undeniable status in the work-world in which he dabbled each day. He knew that his office was indeed a sanctuary in which he could be lord and master of his surrounds, a place where his superior intelligence could be appreciated and respected by colleagues and guests alike.

But that's not all the office meant was it daddy dear?

Arthur lived those latter years in a haze of self-centred deception where the manifestations of his delusions of grandeur were evident on a daily basis. It was not the real world as Jess would later discover, rather one of sycophantic cloying and back-scratching within those vaulted rooms. It was a world where Arthur excelled, where he could continue his pseudo-English pretences as he sat and lectured with pipe in hand and a wry grin of superiority bedecking his face as he gazed at his students.

But it was also a world which denied him the one promotion he desperately needed at the end, wasn't it?

The glimpses that Jess got of her father's sense of his own importance stuck with her throughout her childhood and perhaps beyond. The evening ritual of the silk smoking jacket. The wardrobe full of expensive clothes. The investment in special art offers and memorabilia. And of course the occasional lavish entertaining at home with colleagues.

Hannah of course revelled in any small offerings of grandeur she could pin down and Jess couldn't blame her for that. She thrived on it didn't she? Far more than James or Ruby or Paul.

And certainly far more than me.

Despite that, Jess loved the color and the sights and sounds and smells of those party evenings which were held at home in the Frankston house many years ago. It was all about people and diversity for Jess. Conversation and laughter and music and food, and the rare opportunity to have fun.

That's what I loved.

It was all so *foreign*, and Jess begged to be allowed to stay up and join in the atmosphere of those nights. She recalls now the great variety of people who spoke so many foreign languages and seemed so exotic in their long brightly-colored silk robes. Jess was utterly captivated by them.

See what I mean about a sense of occasion? Knit one purl one knit one . . . .

Bree and Jess are waiting at the tram stop in Fitzroy St. They are growing tired now after wandering around St Kilda and they want to get back home before dark.

The lights change and Jess looks up to see a strange sight. A large woman wearing a red top and a court jester hat is approaching the tram stop. Her hat is black and yellow and red and has tiny brass bells tinkling away on top, and she is carrying a stick wrapped in bright colored velvet in her hand, waving it as she crosses towards us. Atop the stick sits a small court jester doll dressed in the same colors as the bearer. Jess smile and turns away.

The jester-woman pauses and leans against the tram barrier before engaging a man beside them in conversation. They obviously know each other and Jess tries not to listen in. Her mobile phone rings and she pauses mid conversation to answer the call.

Bloody technology I think. How rude!

Get over it Jess I think to myself. Fact of life these days dear.

Jess turns away laughing as she is reminded of the phone gods once more. *Ring bloody ring she thinks. Click buzz whir.*

Bree looks at Jess strangely and says what's got up your goat then dear?

You don't want to know I say. Hahaha.

It occurs to Jess suddenly as she stares at the Toshiba that she is getting side-tracked too often. Stick to the point girl. That's what Arthur would say. No use beating about the bush is there? Out with it!

Jess admonishes herself again for dropping too many stitches in the telling.

Maybe I've dropped whole rows without even realising. Perhaps I should put away the knitting needles for a while and take up some other hobby.

Hahaha.

Hannah took up cross stitch in later life to pass the time but Jess couldn't do it. Too finicky, she couldn't concentrate on all those tiny suckers of stitches. Besides, Jess knows she is far too heavy handed to take up such finery, she doesn't have the motor skills or the patience required so that's that.

I need far more immediate results. Perhaps Hannah didn't.

Ruby surprised everyone by taking up the challenge of knitting but it wasn't like Jess's.

Ruby's knitting was colored and complicated and patterned and she could knit a fairisle jumper in a week which was a miracle in itself. Jess still doesn't know how she did it to this day.

The great pity was of course that the knitting pattern of Ruby's *real* life came unstuck so many times didn't it?

James didn't knit of course, don't be silly he was a boy. But he was the most restless of all and he was rarely still. He could turn his hand to almost anything mechanical and achieved a multitude of tasks, which was just as well really for the livelihood of his family.

Paul dabbled with motor bikes for the short time that he could and Jess always felt that it was ironic that he was riding one at the time of his death.

May used to warn him about it, those things will be the death of you they will she'd say, but of course Paul took no heed.

Who would have predicted that May was right after all? Go figure!

But Jess didn't have hobbies as such, she attacked things seriously and head on. Jess had directions and projects and goals and dreams, she couldn't stand being stuck indoors taking up old-fashioned pastimes. They simply weren't *her*. Instead she pursued sports and outdoor recreation over the years. Hockey, trampolining, swimming, life saving, running, sail boarding, skiing, fishing, sailing, roller blading, camping, basketball.

Jess unleashed her adventurous spark in the years that followed her belated departure from the family home and let her spirit free.

In Jess's final year at high school her parents took a long trip to Europe and America. They were away for three months. It was mainly business for Arthur but not for May, she'd never held a paid job in all the years of their marriage and had been denied the chance to rejoin the workforce. The youngest children were still at school and Jess surmised May must have felt abandoned and bereft stuck at home all day, but Arthur had said no no dear we are doing well now and there is no need for you to work.

Arthur wanted to be the provider and made it clear to May that it was her role to keep the house running smoothly and look after him.

It's simply not done dear he said to May, there is no need for you to work.

May protested weakly and cried for a while about her final loss but she soon got over it and things went back to normal in the family home. Well, as normal as they ever were anyway Jess imagined.

But that's what I mean about disasters and I'm talking with a capital D.

D for defeat as far as May's self-esteem and independence was concerned, washed down the plughole and flushed out to sea. That's where mother's dreams went and not for the first time in her life either. Showed how sensitive to her needs Arthur was, reflected Jess.

So Arthur took May along on the overseas trip as some sort of reparation for his sins. Guilt stuff, Jess realised.

They left mid year when Jess was in the middle of important study and trying to keep up with the demands of matriculation. Arthur didn't encourage his youngest daughter in her studies of course, he thought she was wasting her time.

The older sisters left school sooner Jess he'd told her, and you know you won't need any further study will you. You'll marry some nice young chap and he'll take care of you there there dear, don't waste your time. *See what I mean about sensitivity?*

But Jess wasn't like May. She had strength and stubbornness, so she persisted with her studies.

Despite the lack of parental encouragement, I did it for me.

Ruby and Jess stayed in the Frankston house when Arthur and May left on their trip and Paul stayed with friends. There was a weekly allowance set up for housekeeping and food which the two sisters would often splurge on takeaway and junk food, then they'd be broke till the following week. Jess didn't care though, they were having a great time. Well, mostly anyway.

A taste of independence was what mattered to Jess.

Ruby naturally decided that this was the perfect opportunity to have a few parties and of course Jess felt obliged to go along with her plans.

But Jess didn't enjoy the loudness and drinking and the inevitable mess the next morning, she was still trying to study after all. It annoyed Jess that Ruby was so inconsiderate, but it didn't surprise her one bit, that's how Ruby was.

Jess remembers eating lots of salad sandwiches during that time when her parents were overseas, and perhaps that's because they were easy to prepare. Neither of the girls were good cooks then, and let's face it no wonder. May wasn't the best when it came to culinary skills, so her offspring didn't pick up much either. Perhaps that's why Hannah became such a good cook later in life. To prove to May that *she* could do much better. And wasn't that always the way?

When Arthur and May finally returned home things soon settled back to normal and life went on in the Frankston house. Jess didn't mention Ruby's parties of course but she guessed they suspected, they were young adults after all. Jess was in her eighteenth year and Ruby was almost twenty.

It is a clear crisp Monday morning but it is cold outside. Jess rises early and wanders through to the kitchen. Heater kettle dishes toast. Set the fire, make a mental note to order more wood today. Get the date jar out. Milk from fridge. Margarine peanut butter sugar. Bread from freezer. Running low get more today. Let Mack inside. Collect paper from front lawn. Kettle whistles. Jess settles near the fire with a mug of hot tea and rests her slippered feet on the hearth. Mack plays on the floor and she laughs at his antics as he chases a ball around the table legs, skidding this way and that.

God you're such a bloody dag of a dog Mack, Jess laughs, just as well we love you. Come here boy and I'll give you a bit of my toast.

Spoiled mutt, Jess tells him.

Jess opens the paper and scans the headlines. First the national news to read then world news, but this morning she can't be bothered.

Same old same old I think to myself. Where's the crossword?

Fighting, corruption, and more disasters. With a capital D for sure. Wouldn't you just know it Jess thinks? Welcome to the world on this beautiful sunny winter's morning! Lordy lordy.

Jess knows she is stuck with the news thing, it's part of her make up. The good old news god must have crept into her system somewhere along the line.

Let's face it, I'm a news junkie, can't get enough of it.

Now *that's* a sad fact Jess admits, and she sure as hell doesn't want to analyse why.

Let it be Jess, let it be.

Arthur sure enjoyed his daily news fix too, it was a ritual that he enshrined as part of his homecoming from work and he stuck to it rigidly. The daily paper went with his pipe and slippers and smoking jacket and sherry didn't it? Arthur would sit in the blood red club chair in the lounge with his feet propped on the foot stool and his sherry beside him on the brass table, his face hidden behind the newsprint. Silence would ensue, and they all knew better than to interrupt father at that time of day. It just wasn't done was it?

May would usually join her husband when the evening meal was underway and she would have a sherry too. Just a small one dear thank you dear she'd say, I have to go and check on the tea you know.

But she couldn't have checked too often, it was always overcooked and bland. Meat and three veg, you know the sort of meal I'm talking about. The standard Aussie meal of the post war era, at least in Jess's house it was. May would always add salt and sugar to the peas.

Yuk. Unthinkable now.

For some strange reason Jess recalls two dishes that May cooked, Sea Pie and Dutch Ragout. Both equally tasteless and a picture of visual suicide as far as Jess and her siblings were concerned. Even May probably didn't enjoy the consumption of her regular attempts at gastronomy, but she persevered because they were her creations after all.

Arthur's mother had been an excellent cook in her day, so most likely he probably suffered May's cooking with disdain, though he was always complimentary and diplomatic.

Arthur had no choice, it was a trade-off for the deprivations poor May endured in other areas of their long-standing marriage, and he realised that at least there was food on the table each evening.

Be damned if he'd ever stoop to cooking, not men's work, eh?

When it came to celebrations or functions of any sort though May found that extra something and actually excelled herself in the kitchen from time to time. Her productions were not without hassles and hiccups of course, but impressive nonetheless. Jess recalls the soirees for Arthur's work colleagues where May prepared platters of horse d'oeuvres and finger foods. Dips and crackers and pastries, that sort of thing.

But Jess loved those nights when she was allowed to stay up late and play waitress. She relished the chance to mingle and chat and the food was of little consequence. It was the *occasion* that Jess adored.

Years later when she was older and living by herself in the big Frankston house May streamlined her cooking to a minimum, which was probably just as well. She often forgot that she'd even put the stove on and wander outside to her beloved garden, and the blackened wallpaper in the kitchen bore testimony to some of the frequent battles May had with pots and pans left unattended. It's just as well she preferred salads and rice biscuits and sea food that didn't need cooking.

But eggs were also a favourite and of course they needed cooking of some sort didn't they?

May also loved oysters and would buy half a dozen when she could manage to get them. I suppose it was in her genes, the sea god connection. She would often eat them out in the garden then put the empty shells around her orchid pots.

It keeps the snails and slugs out she would tell Jess, better than weed killer she'd say.

And who was I to argue?

May sure had a way with plants, she was a veritable green thumb, and her garden was a testimony to her skills. She planted vegetables every year right up to the end. Spinach, lettuce, tomatoes. May spent most of her waking hours out turning over the soil, digging and potting, watering and weeding. She always joked that that's how she wanted to go.

To die in the garden with her boots on.

She didn't quite make it in the end but at least she was close.

Jess is mid sentence when the phone rings, a friend from the city.

Hi she says, what's happening?

The usual Jess replies, what about you? What have you been doing lately?

Well last week I spent a day and a half downloading broadband she replies. Bigpond. You wouldn't believe it she says, modern technology. Isn't it marvellous?

Bloody oath Jess laughs, that's progress for you dear!

Well, replies her friend, it's a pain I can tell you! I've lost all my email addresses, and to top it all off the bloody computer isn't much faster than before.

Jesus Joseph and Mary, Jess screams down the phone between laughs, you should have just stayed with the old system. Now the damn Bigpond god has eaten all your contacts hahaha.

What's yours by the way Jess, she asks?

My what?

Email stupid, she says. Honestly Jess, it's enough to make you cry. Where have all those names gone? I don't know, they must be somewhere in the system but I can't retrieve them. My daughter could probably fix it for me but she's in Sydney so that's not much help.

Damn right Jess agrees, besides dear you should know the golden rule about offspring and computers. Never let them near the damn things under any circumstances!

Last time number one son fixed mine I no longer recognised the screen. What's happened I asked him in a state of shock, why is it all different?

I've re-configured it mum to make it easier to use, he sighed patiently, as though Jess was asking him if the sky had fallen since she last looked out the window.

Easier to use, Jess shouted back, who for? I don't recognise my own computer any more Jess responded ungratefully.

Number one son just let out a long deliberate sigh down the phone as though there was nothing more he could do to save his own mother from the wonders of the computer, Jess tells her friend, I was a lost cause as far as he was concerned and didn't I just know it.

And then there was the time when I lent the laptop to my daughter, Jess continues. Well at least I got it back, but the trouble was the damn thing was in hibernation mode. True, Jess says, couldn't get so much as a flicker from the damn thing.

Are you serious Jess, her friend yells down the phone? I thought only bears went into hibernation in winter she laughs, so what happened to the laptop then?

I had to recharge the battery and eventually the thing woke up, Jess snorts. It finally started working again didn't it? Hahahaha. You just wouldn't believe it would you, Jess guffaws?

The whole world has gone mad, her friend screams back, and now they are both in fits of laughter, and that goes for the English language as well.

Too right Jess exclaims, and you know how much I worship the word gods! Now we have computer speak and sms speak and emails jetting round the globe so fast that it makes my head spin just thinking about it all Jess finishes.

Computers have hibernation and mice and bytes and blogs and viruses, it's all too much, Jess yells, too bloody much! The world wide web has a lot to answer for and that's another thing, why do they use a term relating to spiders?

I guess because we're all trapped in it whether we like it or not, my friend reasons, it's a done deal that's for sure.

www Jess replies. World weary warrior, that's how I feel about technology, whoever said it makes life easy?

Jess checks her daily emails and clicks on the one from a friend in China. There is a clip attachment but she can't be bothered to download it right now, too many other things waiting for attention this morning. It will have to sit in the inbox for a while.

Bree calls out from the kitchen, want a coffee Jess and by the way have you checked the emails yet?

Jess laughs as she clicks on the exit box and leaves the computer for a bit. The pictures of China can wait, I'll send some replies later today when I've finished other tasks Jess decides.

Get back on that ol' web. www.

Have you noticed how our whole language structure has had to change to adapt to technology Jess asks as they sip their coffee at the kitchen table? Mostly we don't even use capital letters any more. Sorry, upper case.

It's all lower case these days observes Bree, people just don't have the time to hold down the shift or caps lock do they?

See what I mean about the techno stuff replies Jess, it's gone berserk! Poor May would turn in her grave, she was such a stickler for grammar and correct word usage and pronunciation. She'd be horrified now wouldn't she? Just as well she's gone, god rest her.

Too right replies Bree, when I learned English at school shift meant to move something didn't it?

Jess looks across at her strangely. You should know Bree, we've shifted often enough haven't we hahaha? Now shift is a plastic tab on the computer keyboard with an arrow pointing skywards, what's that about, Jess asks?

Maybe we're all shifting upwards to somewhere in the universe laughs Bree. You know Jess, it's all about the big picture these days and I suppose we all have to shift in some way or another.

Shift our bloody mindset that's for sure Jess adds. Hahaha.

God Jess you're such a baby boomer Bree replies, and they both fall about in fits of laughter as they finish their coffee.

What about caps lock then says Jess? How on earth can you lock a cap, it doesn't make sense hahaha?

Well at least it brings up some sort of mental image says Bree, not like num lock, what's that about?

Damned if I know Jess replies, but the whole thing makes me numb that's for sure. I think my favourites though have got to be Power Sleep and Wake Up, even May would understand those but it's a bit too late for her isn't it? She sure doesn't need the computer gods now.

Anyway you look at it says Bree, there's no getting away from technology now is there? We're stuck with it Jess, so deal with it okay?

Deal with it? Sure thing, why if it wasn't for the daily dose of fun with all the techno gods where would I be? Hahaha.

The matriculation results came out in the early morning paper. The milk train brought them to Frankston station at about 5.30a.m., and Jess remembers swinging on the white wooden boom gate while she waited.

It was such a big thing and Jess was so nervous.

It was an entry to her future despite the fact that Jess didn't really know if she was ready.

Jess desperately wanted to pass to prove to Arthur she was a success. Jess had worked hard to prove a point, to equal James and go one better than both Hannah and Ruby.

When the paper finally arrived and Jess found her results it was only a Comp pass.

Maybe I'm just a small c kid after all Jess thought bitterly.

But it was a pass nonetheless and she was pretty happy with that.

She'd done it hadn't she, passed her final year of high school and achieved a ticket to tertiary studies and independence. Yahoo!

The noise at the station boomed as hoots and whistles and joy and hugs and tears and frustration and anger erupted. There were shouts of excitement and congratulations and commiserations. It seemed for a short space of time that all that mattered in the world were those few printed letters beside your name in the pages of the morning newspaper.

Nothing else seemed relevant right then did it?

Jess didn't notice the cold or the time or the sunrise or the trains or the early morning shift workers. All that she knew was that somehow her life would never be the same again.

Would it?

They bought some wool yesterday for Bree. I want to knit a scarf she tells me over dinner, what do you think?

Good idea, Jess says, we'll get some wool tomorrow when we're up the street. Better get needles too, I don't know if my old ones are still around.

Knit one purl one, knit one ... whoops!

They're in the sewing shop looking at wool and Jess asks the young shop assistant for help in selecting the needles they'll need.

I haven't knitted anything for ages Jess tells her, not since my children were little. Now I'm having grandchildren, Jess laughs.

Well that's a few generations ago the young thing replies tartly as she scans Jess's face. You'll probably want to start knitting for the grandchild she says.

A few generations Jess bleats, not bloody likely!

I don't think I'll take up knitting again at this stage Jess snorts indignantly, besides who wears wool any more? It's all polar fleece these days isn't it, you should know that.

But the young thing doesn't turn a hair, Jess's sarcasm must have missed the mark.

You'd be surprised, she responds.

Wouldn't I just, thinks Jess!

Bree and Jess pay for the wool and needles then cross the road to their favourite coffee shop. Fancy a coffee and toasted bun Bree asks?

I'd kill for one Jess replies, as long as the waitress is over fourteen and knows how to make a decent latte, hahaha.

Settle down says Bree, just because you used to work in a bakery in the holidays. Not everyone's hopeless Jess you know.

Jess ignores her and lines up at the counter with her coffee card in hand.

The usual, she says to the waitress.

Toasted scroll with that?

Sure, Jess repies, and don't forget the jug of cold milk with the coffees will you?

Jess takes the table number she's offered and joins Bree at their regular table by the window.

God Jess you're so predictable Bree says, that's what I like about you. I could set my clock by your daily routines hahaha.

I know I know, Jess replies, I can't help it, I'm a creature of habit. Not sure where I got that from either but I'm stuck with it now Jess adds. Still, it could be worse, James and Paul weren't methodical or organised like me and look what happened to them!

You can't help bad timing replies Bree, maybe it's the boy thing.

Well I don't know about that, Jess responds, there's timing and there's choices and perhaps they messed up both those things didn't they?

But Bree has lost interest in Jess's musing and who could blame her really?

I'll have to stop rabbiting on about the past Jess reminds herself, it does nothing to help the present or the future does it?

They are tearing down the old back fence in readiness for the new one. Jess knows it has to go of course, but still it's a pity.

I liked the old one, it went with the house.

And besides, now they'll lose the only tree left in the small back yard.

Oh well says Bree, never mind, we'll plant some natives. It'll be just like our garden on the island she says. They'll attract the birds too, you'll see.

I'm sure new trees will be great Jess replies, but they won't be a decent height for a few years yet and that's the trouble.

Well dear you can't have it all ways says Bree, as though that's somehow the end of the conversation.

But Jess is not convinced, she knows that this summer they'll be stuck gazing at the new brick house just the other side of the fence.

Oh well, that's progress for you, can't beat it can you?

Let's have lunch then Jess says to Bree, bugger the fence.

Jess collects the mail as she returns from walking Mack. Just one solitary piece of mail today, a letter from Telstra.

Uh oh Jess thinks, here we go again. Someone has re-activated the Telstra god when I wasn't looking.

She throws the letter down on the kitchen table and prepares a late lunch. Re-heated sausage rolls from yesterday.

The Telstra gods can wait, I'm hungry.

Finally Jess opens the letter as she sips another coffee.

Dear Jess, we are writing to advise you of some changes to your hotline plan blah blah blah.

Hotline plan I shriek as I nearly spill the coffee. What hotline plan? I'm with Optus and I should know they charge me enough don't they?

Jess decides to phone the 1800 number and try to sort all this out once more, but she doesn't have the energy to do it straight away.

It's just too much right now, too darned much! Besides, Jess is the last person who would be even slightly interested in the fine print, what the hell does she want with capped calls and community calls and Advanced Plans and Reward Options?

Tell someone who cares Jess screams at noone in particular, I've had it!

After lunch Jess drives into town to meet Bree for coffee.

I think I'm losing the plot, Jess mumbles into her coffee.

What plot Bree asks, not the book surely?

No, just life in general, Bree moans before telling her about the Telstra letter.

I don't understand why I'm still on their mailing system Jess explains, surely that's what computers are for isn't it? You'd thing someone would have pressed the delete button by now wouldn't you Jess wails?

Maybe that's what you should do Jess with all this techno crap, just delete it from your daily existence for a while. Get rid of it. Don't press the start button dear and chill out for a while. I think it's getting to you says Bree.

Perhaps you're right, but then where would I be asks Jess? If I didn't have my laptop and mobile and the cordless phone how would I communicate with the outside world?

But that's my point dear, you need some time out don't you think replies Bree sympathetically? It's getting to you Jess and even I can see that, you're becoming a bit obsessed with it all. Who needs it? Give it the flick for a while.

Jess drives home musing over what Bree said and it makes sense.

I don't really need to be in the loop at the moment do I?

Back home, Jess decides to call her daughter overseas. It's her day off, but of course she doesn't answer and Jess gets a message instead.

The Vodaphone you have called is currently switched off. Please try again later.

Aaaagh! Now the Vodaphone gods are talking too.

Jess presses the stop button and realises that Bree is right, it's time she switched off too and became unavailable.

I'm sure I can do it. Piece of cake!

Jess flicks off the computer and the mobile and sits down in her favourite chair with Mack on her knee. Now what time does the news start again?

Jess had decided to have her twenty first birthday at the Frankston house. She'd moved back there after a brief spell living in Melbourne, so it seemed the easy option. Arthur and May actually agreed, so Jess went ahead with the plans.

It was a small guest list of mainly high school and college friends, about thirty in all. Arthur supplied the drinks and May put in an all out effort with the food. Jess was on a studentship at the time, so she was grateful for any expenses saved. She had been pleasantly surprised by her parents decision to allow the party at all.

There's no accounting for some things is there?

Jess wore a lime green pleated linen dress with a white V necked collar, which she'd purchased on layby. It was very smart and very short and left a hell of a lot of leg showing, but that was the fashion of the time. Jess wore white fish net stockings and patent leather heels to complete the outfit, and thought she looked pretty fabulous at the time.

Her hair was short and Jess curled it with rollers for the occasion, then covered it with enough hair spray to completely melt a whole section of the ozone layer.

We didn't know about such harmful things then of course. Like cigarettes and sunbaking and binge drinking.

Besides everyone did it darling, didn't they?

Be cool, have another ciggie Jess that's the way. Here's your cinzano and lemonade too. Down the hatch. Drink it down down down down, skol! Hurrah!

Happy birthday to you, Happy birthday to you . . . .

By the time the midnight celebration and speeches came round Jess was pretty drunk, they all were. Off their faces, plastered.

But geez we were having the best of times weren't we?

The last thing Jess recalls about the evening was when Arthur came through to the loungeroom at around 1.30a.m. to break it up and send the guests home. He'd had enough and who could blame him? There was his youngest daughter dancing on the couch and throwing talcum powder over everyone while the Beach Boys played at top volume on the corner stereo. We must have all looked like zombies, Jess recalls.

Can I talk to you Jess, Arthur had said between gritted teeth as he stood in the hallway in his dressing gown, I think it's time we called it a night don't you? Your mother and I would like to get some sleep.

But I'm having such fun daddykins and don't you just feel the love?

However all Arthur felt was anger and annoyance, and he insisted that the party was over. Finito. Kaput!

So Jess reluctantly called it a night and showed the guests out. As she shut the front door behind them it scraped on broken glass in the hallway. *Twenty one today, she's got the key to the door . . . . what a mess!*

It is a dull and overcast Wednesday morning and the wood truck has arrived. Jess meets the driver outside and shows him where to dump the load. A cubic metre of red gum spews noisily from the dump truck as Jess watches over the fence.

She feels a twinge of guilt as she hauls the logs into the backyard.

Maybe I'm adding to the greenhouse effect by burning fossil fuels. Maybe I'm responsible for depleting vital red gum forests and whole eco systems, who knows? I don't.

But whichever way you look at it Jess figures, we have to get our heat from *somewhere* don't we? We're not burning gas or using electricity for heating so perhaps that's a plus, isn't it?

Jess tries to ignore the small electric heater in her office and the power it uses, she has to stay warm somehow after all.

Bugger the consequences of global warming Jess thinks as she stacks the wood by the back door, it's my own warming that concerns me right now! That's probably being selfish, but what can you do? We can't sit in a cold house all winter with blankets over our knees to keep warm can we, Jess reasons?

But Jess feels guilty just thinking about all the people out there who do just that because they can't afford heating. And what about the homeless? Aaagh!

Jess switches off the guilt button as she finishes stacking the woodpile. *It's doing my head in.*

She puts the wheelbarrow away and goes back inside to the warm kitchen. A nice cup of green tea that's what you need Jess, she tells herself. That won't harm the environment will it?

Now where did I put that teapot?

Jess is sitting quietly on the couch in the den when Bree arrives home from work. Tea is cooked and the dog has been walked and fed. The house is clean and the dishes put away.

I'm waiting for something but I don't know what. Knit one purl one . . . .

Hi there Jess, how's things, asks Bree? How was your day?

I think I've reached the end I tell her.

End of what Bree says, your tether?

The book, Jess responds. I think it's finished, but I'm not sure. I feel like I'm just going through the motions at the moment, Jess adds, treading water. You know how it is.

Perhaps you need a break from it dear, Bree replies as she stoops down to pat Mack, I can see it's doing you in and that's no good Jess. Give it a rest for a bit why don't you?

A big rest or a little rest Jess asks?

How should I know replies Bree, it's your baby dear.

Baby. Baby baby baby. There it is again.

It's that word the sisters used all those years ago isn't it, when Jess was the little sister.

Baby baby you're just a baby hahaha.

The words and the taunts and the demands and the songs echo round and round in her skull.

Jess feels the pull of the tide dragging her back to the seas of her childhood once more. She is floating further and further away from the shore where they wait. Those sisters, Hannah and Ruby. It is *them*.

I know yes I know who you are.

Jess drifts on the tide, warmed by the aqua saltspray. The sun glows through her as she is caught in a place without time. It is beautiful. It is *her* world, not theirs, a space Jess has created on her own. It becomes a whole galaxy, a world of words.

See see what I have made, come and look!

With sudden clarity Jess realises that she doesn't need them any more. The sisters are banished to another place beyond her world and Jess wonders why it took her so long to do it. The eviction, the line crossed in the sand.

Sometimes it takes only a moment in time to achieve extraordinary things, and for Jess that's how it was.

A click of the delete button was all it took, that's how simple it was in the end.

And I should know.

Jess picks up May's tortoiseshell knitting needles and a smile bubbles to the surface as she resumes the knitting.

Knit one purl one knit one purl one . . . .

I'm not the little sister any more.